"I don't think I can

He stared at her mouth, wanting to part her lips with his. To taste her again. "Do what?"

"Be a good aunt or a good mom." Her chin trembled. "Matthew's right. I don't know the first thing about him, Emma or Sophia. I don't have a clue how to reach them."

This was his chance. The moment he'd been hoping for when he'd invited her to stay with them, and it had come much sooner than he'd expected. All he had to do was agree, reassure her the kids were better off with him, then she'd leave next week.

But that would also leave the kids with one less dependable adult in their lives. Another loss of someone who loved them.

Landon wished he could remain silent, watch Katie fail at being a good parent and not feel guilty. Only, it wasn't about what he wanted—it was about Matthew, Emma and Sophia.

"Instead of using your head," he whispered, "use your heart."

Dear Reader,

At some point during our childhood, we're asked: *What do you want to be when you grow up?* Some people know exactly what they want out of life and have a bold, confident answer to that question.

Katie Richards isn't one of those people.

Coming home has never been easy for Katie. She's always stood out in the small mountain town of Elk Valley—and not in a good way. She's headstrong, impulsive and unsure of what she wants out of life. And she's just lost the person she loves most in the world: her sister.

Landon Eason knows exactly who he is: mature, responsible and the kind of man you can count on for anything. Which is why it's no surprise to him that his childhood friend, Katie's sister, named him guardian of her three children. Only, he hadn't counted on Katie being designated as primary guardian, and he's terrified of losing three children he's grown to love as his own.

In *Tennessee Homecoming*, Katie discovers what she really wants out of life and Landon is left with a difficult decision to make. Because helping Katie find happiness may cost him his own.

As always, thank you for reading.

April

HOME *on the* RANCH
TENNESSEE HOMECOMING

——— ✂ ———

APRIL
ARRINGTON

H **HARLEQUIN**® HOME ON THE RANCH

Recycling programs
for this product may
not exist in your area.

ISBN-13: 978-1-335-54300-4
ISBN-13: 978-1-335-63399-6 (Direct to Consumer edition)

Home on the Ranch: Tennessee Homecoming

Printed in U.S.A.

www.Harlequin.com

April Arrington grew up in a small Southern town and developed a love for movies and books at an early age. Emotionally moving stories have always held a special place in her heart. April enjoys collecting pottery and soaking up the Georgia sun on her front porch.

Books by April Arrington

Home on the Ranch: Tennessee Bull Rider

Harlequin Western Romance

Elk Valley, Tennessee

A Home with the Rancher

Men of Raintree Ranch

Twins for the Bull Rider
The Rancher's Wife
The Bull Rider's Cowgirl
The Rancher's Miracle Baby

Visit the Author Profile page
at Harlequin.com for more titles.

Dedicated to Johanna Raisanen.
The best teachers have a skilled eye, great advice and a good sense of humor. I've learned so much from you. Thank you for being such an awesome editor and helping me grow as a writer!

Chapter 1

Landon Eason always found a sound, logical answer to every question, but this particularly painful answer eluded him.

"Why?" A shaky feminine voice pitched higher at his back. "Why leave them to her? Why not me? I'm their grandm—"

A choked sob then silence followed.

Landon stared out the bay window of Patricia Richards's stately home, a burning sensation heating his chest and pricking his eyes. Blinking hard, he focused on the two children sitting outside on the wide porch swing. Matthew, ten, stared down at his dark dress shoes as they dragged across the floor with each slow movement of the swing. His five-year-old sister, Emma, leaned against him, tears rolling down her cheeks, soaking the lacy collar of her black dress.

Any other day the two of them would be tearing across the sprawling green fields, splashing in nearby mountain streams and soaking up the Tennessee sun. It was a perfect day in Elk Valley for play—warm air, blue sky, strong budding trees to climb—but Matthew and Emma weren't interested.

They had good reason not to be.

"I'm their grandmother," Patricia continued firmly. "I was the one who held Jennifer's hand each time she gave birth. I was the first one to see them, to hear them cry. And you've always been there for Frank and these kids, Landon—*always*. How could they do it? How could they name you second to Katie? How could they just cut us out of their lives and hand them over to her?"

How? Throat tight, Landon gentled his grip on the small bundle in his arms and faced Patricia. Hell, he didn't know how Frank and Jennifer had made the decision regarding guardianship of their three children. Or why. All he knew was the wrinkled papers trembling in Patricia's clenched fist had the power to take away three kids he'd grown to love as his own over the years, their cute faces and familiar voices the only tangible reminders left of his two best friends.

"I can count on one hand the number of occasions Katie has spent time with them," Patricia continued, "and she doesn't know the first thing about being a parent. Not to mention she never follows through with anything. She left here to pursue a singing career but pitched that after less than a year to take up bartending. Then it was landscaping, and now she's in marketing— for however long that will last. She's not dependable enough to be trusted with children." Mascara streaked her powdered cheeks. Patricia shook her head, a gray curl slipping from her elegant topknot as she looked toward Emma and Matthew. "She's unfit."

She's also your daughter. Landon bit his tongue and looked away. Why Patricia held such disdain for Katie still confused and shocked him. Yes, Katie had been levelheaded Jennifer's opposite in her teenaged years and probably gave stiff-upper-lip Patricia hell. And no, Katie wasn't equipped to be any kid's guardian. But did that justify Patricia damn near disowning her?

Maybe Patricia's resentment was rooted in the fact that Katie rarely returned to her hometown of Elk Valley—or, perhaps, it was the way she'd gone about leaving.

He remembered the day Katie left. While Jennifer had graduated as valedictorian of her and Landon's class, Katie, eighteen, five years younger than Jennifer and ten times more outspoken, had scrambled onto the football field at the last second, last to be seated, last to receive her diploma and last in academic achievements. The moment after she'd tossed her graduation cap in the air, Katie had jogged to the parking lot, hopped in a car stuffed with bulging suitcases and peeled out of Elk Valley. Her car's sporadic skid marks clung to the cracked pavement in the parking lot throughout the ten years since she'd left.

If Landon drove to that parking lot today, the muscle memory in his hands and feet would know exactly where to turn his truck's steering wheel and press the brake to catch a glimpse of their faded outline.

The thought stirred a sick sensation in his gut. That was it most likely. That disgusting hollow Katie had left behind in those who'd cared about her—Jennifer, Patricia and…him.

"She won't agree to it," Landon said. "When she finds out, she'll sign over her rights to the kids then go back to California."

Patricia relaxed slightly. "And they'll stay here with us."

"That's the plan."

At times, Patricia wasn't the easiest person in the world to get along with, but if he had to share custody with either her or Katie, Patricia was the better choice and, altogether, the best scenario for the kids. At least, he supposed—his throat tightening—in the absence of their parents.

"We'll proceed with moving the children's things to your ranch tomorrow morning." Patricia hesitated. "I think it's a good idea if they stay here with me tonight. That is, if you agree?"

He nodded. "Sophia's room is already set up but that'll give me time to finish clearing out the bedrooms for Matthew and Emma tonight."

A whimper emerged from within Landon's arms and small feet thumped his abs. He glanced down at the little bundle cradled against him and smoothed a hand over the baby's back. Brown curls snagged on the stubble lining his jaw as Sophia, Jennifer and Frank's six-month-old daughter, nuzzled her face against his neck then settled back into sleep. The small pink rose on her thin headband—an accessory Jennifer had added to the baby's outfits daily—slipped behind her left ear.

Three nights ago, Sophia had been asleep in the crib he'd made for her when Patricia had called to give him the awful news. It'd been almost impossible to believe. Just hours earlier, Jennifer and Frank had smiled, waved, then gotten in their car and driven away from his ranch. It was supposed to be a romantic getaway for Jennifer and Frank and another fun-filled weekend of babysitting for him. There'd been sunshine, blue sky and the scent of honeysuckle on the breeze.

There hadn't been a single sign of what was to come. Not of the woman in oncoming traffic eighty miles down the road who stole glances at her cell phone, and texted her teenaged daughter as she drove. Not of Frank's carefree speed that accelerated a bit more the closer he and Jennifer drew to their relaxing destination. And certainly not of the sharp mountain curve where both drivers would collide, ending all of their lives before the tires stopped spinning on the overturned vehicles.

Telling the children the news had been the hardest thing he'd ever had to do and though Sophia was too young to be told or comprehend, she'd cried more often the past three days. As though instinctively, she knew something had changed. As though she somehow felt the loss.

"Would you like me to take her?" Voice thin, Patricia tossed the papers she held on to the coffee table then crossed the living room with outstretched arms. "I could put her down for a nap in my room."

"No." Eyes blurring at the reminder of their loss, Landon faced the window again and hugged Sophia closer. She made a sound of contentment, the rhythmic puff of her warm breath and healthy beat of her heart against the base of his throat easing the tremor in his limbs. "She won't have time to settle. We need to head out soon."

Patricia sniffed. "If Katie isn't here within the next ten minutes, we're leaving without her." Her high heels clicked across the gleaming hardwood floor, and a sharp edge returned to her tone. "I won't be late to my own daughter's funeral."

As if on cue, a dusty red sports car growled down the long graveled driveway. It slowed as it neared the circular end, then stopped beside his truck. Landon eased closer to the window, narrowed his eyes and waited.

The car's windows were tinted too darkly to see inside and the doors remained closed. A good five minutes passed and still no one emerged from the vehicle.

Landon guessed it was Katie sitting in the car. Who knew what she was driving now. Jennifer had told him she changed vehicles as often as some people changed their oil—though with her family's wealth she could afford to do so—and it'd been two years since he'd last seen her. During her most recent visit home one year ago, Katie had stayed only one day, arriving and leaving town before he had had a chance to catch a glimpse of her. And she hadn't returned to Elk Valley at all for Sophia's birth—a fact Jennifer had lowered her eyes and sighed over each of the many times Patricia had mentioned it.

"It's about time." Patricia, makeup repaired and composure regained, returned to his side and looked out the window. She frowned. "Why is she just sitting there?" Her silk sleeve brushed his arm as she headed for the door, heels clacking. "Doesn't she know the wake starts in half an hour?"

"Patricia." Landon touched her elbow and gestured toward Sophia. "Why don't you take Sophia and I'll check on Katie? Is Harold ready?"

She hesitated, nodding absently as her eyes darted from Sophia to the red car then upstairs. "He's putting on his tie now. He—" Her voice cracked. "He's having a hard time. I hope you don't mind, but I think it'd help if you and the children rode with us."

"And Katie, too?" Landon asked softly. "I know you have your differences but I imagine she's hurting as much as Harold, and the kids could use all the support they can get. On the way out, if you'd like me to, I could ask David to bring the car around."

Patricia stared at Katie's car then nodded stiffly and reached for Sophia.

Landon helped settle Sophia into Patricia's arms, made a quick call to David, Patricia's driver, to request the limo then walked to the front porch. Early-afternoon sunlight glared down at him just beneath the porch's roof and he threw up his hand to shield it.

"Is that her?" Matthew had stopped the swing, planted his feet on the floor and pinned his narrowed gaze on the red car. "She actually showed?"

Landon studied the muscle flickering in Matthew's jaw and the tight grip of his hand around the swing's armrest. "Yeah."

"She never bothered coming before," Matthew bit out. "Why's she here now?"

Emma sat up and rubbed her wet cheeks. "Why's who here now?"

"Your aunt Katie," Landon said gently.

Expression brightening, Emma glanced at the driveway. "Can I go see her?"

"Soon," Landon said. "Matthew, would you please take Emma inside and help your grandmother get Sophia's bag together? We're leaving soon and we're gonna ride with your grandparents."

Matthew scowled and jerked his chin toward the driveway. "Is she riding with us, too?"

Landon walked over and crouched in front of them. "I think it'll help us all feel better—especially your grandparents—to go together."

"You mean Gammie won't cry anymore if we ride with her?" Emma blinked up at him, her lips trembling.

Landon managed a strained smile. Man, he wished he could take this hardship away from them. Wished he could put his hand out, roll back the clock and edge Frank's truck two inches to the left at just the right second. Or at the very least, tell a white lie and ease their grief. But reality—painful or joyful—had to be faced, and in his opinion, obscuring the truth never made dealing with it any better.

"She'll still cry, Emma," he said. "We all will. But it won't hurt as much if she has you and Matthew nearby."

Emma's brow furrowed as she pondered this then she nodded matter-of-factly. "I'll hold her hand."

"Thank you, sweetheart." Landon helped her down from the swing, kissed her forehead then looked at Matthew. "How 'bout it, buddy? Will you help me out?"

He shrugged stiffly, cast one last sour look at the red car then trudged inside.

Landon stood and stared at the darkened car windows. His flesh tingled and he balled his hands into fists at his side. Of all the occasions he'd imagined seeing Katie again, none of them had involved these circumstances.

He hated this day. Every damned second of it.

Forcing himself to move, he approached the vehicle. He stopped by the driver's-side door then knocked on the dusty window. "Katie?"

Muffled sounds emerged. The catch of breath? A sob, maybe? "I—I'll be out in a minute."

"Hey." He dragged his hands over his thighs, the smooth material of his dress pants wrinkling beneath his touch. "Everyone's waiting for you. Why don't you come on out and ride to the church with us?"

The quiet sounds from inside the car stopped; only the chirps of birds and soft whistle of the cool breeze rustling trees filled the air.

Landon's shoulders sagged. It wasn't like Katie to hide out or avoid trying situations. For as long as he'd known her, she'd been headstrong, vivacious and defiant of fate. But then again, she'd never experienced a loss like this.

"Katie?" He tried for a laugh, the nervous sound making even him cringe. "You're not gonna leave me to ride with Patricia on my own, are you?" His boots scraped across the paved driveway as he shifted from one foot to the other. "I know we egg each other on from time to time but that'd be taking it to a new level."

The door clicked then slowly opened.

Landon stepped back, a calming warmth spreading through his chest as her long limbs and dark curls emerged from the car. She straightened to her full height—all six feet of lithe, graceful strength accentuated by soft curves—and faced him. Black sunglasses shielded her eyes, a red flush stamped her cheeks and the smooth contours of her kissable mouth shook.

"It's been a while." His voice was husky. He cleared his throat then tried again. "You wanna take those glasses off so I can say hello properly?"

She didn't speak. Her shaky hand curled tighter around the frame of the car door, the metallic silver polish on her nails sparkling in the sunlight. A tear rolled out from beneath the thick bottom frame of her sunglasses then trickled down her face in an erratic pattern.

Hesitating, he reached out, touched the bridge of her glasses with a fingertip then nudged them down her nose. Her thick lashes lifted and those beautiful browns of hers focused up at him, the dark depths heavy with pain, the surrounding whites cloaked in a pink haze.

"I was getting myself together." She dragged the back of her hand across her cheek. "I didn't want to upset Matthew and Emma after what they've already been through. I haven't seen them in so long, and I didn't want to make the day more difficult for you, either. I'm sorry. I know you and Frank were as close as me and…"

Her chin wobbled and a fresh trail of tears coursed over her skin.

"Katie." His tongue barely moved, her name escaping his lips on a strained whisper that made his whole body ache.

Against his better judgment, he spread his arms, palms tilted up in invitation. She released the car door, moved into his embrace and pressed her cheek to his chest. The sharp hinge of her sunglasses dug into the base of his

throat but the sweet scent of her hair—*strawberries*—
and the sun-kissed warmth of her smooth skin coaxed
him into holding her closer. Her heart pounded against
his chest in almost the same place Sophia's had.

Landon winced. Katie had never set eyes on Sophia.
How would she react to the news? And how much would
it hurt for her to sign away guardianship of her nieces
and nephew? Not as much as it would for someone else
in her position, for sure. She barely knew the kids and
Patricia had been shockingly accurate in her estimation
of how much time Katie had actually spent with them.

But the last thing he wanted to do was add to her
pain. Surely there'd be a better moment to tell her. To
gently explain why Matthew, Emma and Sophia would
be better off here with him and Patricia, and reassure
her that she'd always be welcome in the kids' lives. For
now, offering comfort superseded everything.

Landon released a heavy breath, ruffling errant
strands of her silky hair against his nose. "We're glad
you came home for the funeral. Before you leave, we
need to—"

"I'm not here just for the funeral."

He froze. Did she already know? "What?"

Katie raised her head from his chest, stepped back
then plucked the sunglasses off her nose. The tears had
stopped, determination warring with the grief still shad-
owing her eyes. "I'm here for the kids."

Buck up, Katydid. There's nothing you can't handle.
Throat tight at the memory of Jennifer's words, Katie
hung her sunglasses on her pants pocket then peered
up at Landon. Sharp rays of sunlight beat down on her

burning eyes, and made it difficult to discern Landon's reaction to her announcement.

She shifted until his towering height blocked the glare. It didn't help. If anything, a clear view of his face—as handsome as ever—only increased her tension.

"I came for an extended visit to help Matthew and Emma through this," she said. "My dad, too, and—" *Lord knows if she'll accept it* "—my mom. I didn't want you to think I was just blowing in and out of here like I have before."

His blue eyes narrowed and a muscle ticked in his strong, stubble-lined jaw. The heat of his consoling touch still lingered on her thin blouse, seeping through to her shoulders and lower back. The delicious sensation tingled against her skin.

He'd held her once before—years ago at Jennifer and Frank's wedding—in much the same way. As maid of honor, she'd spent the hours before the wedding applying Jennifer's makeup, smoothing her long hair and fluffing the train of her wedding dress. During the ceremony, she'd stood by Jennifer's side, praying silently for a happy future for Jennifer and Frank, then smiled bravely as they'd walked arm in arm back up the aisle, down the front steps of Elk Valley Baptist Church then slid into a white limo idling by the curb.

She'd continued smiling as Jennifer had waved from the back window. Her beaming parents and a slew of guests had followed the newlyweds for over a block, cheering and laughing. But the farther the distance, the more Katie had struggled to smile, her heart breaking, feeling as though Jennifer—her older sister, best friend and confidante—had left her behind.

It'd been selfish, really, and she'd never felt more ashamed. When Landon had looked at her—the two of them, best man and maid of honor, the only ones still standing on the church steps—she'd known it must've shown on her face. She'd expected a look of admonishment or a few words of disapproval. Instead, he'd called her name, opened his arms then held her while she'd cried.

Katie swallowed hard, choking back a renewed sob. "I reserved a room at the Elk Valley Motel on the way through town. Paid for a week in advance."

Landon relaxed. One corner of his sensuous mouth curved up as he slid his big hands in his pockets. "You're staying for one week?"

She nodded. "A little longer if they'll accept my help."

"That's good, then." He looked away, his thick blond hair tumbling over his tanned brow as he stared over her shoulder.

Landon hadn't changed much except for a brawnier build and more noticeable lines beside his mouth that deepened into grooves when he smiled. Laugh lines. He'd always been optimistic, cheerful and fun-natured, even if his high standards were a bit rigid and legalistic. His blue eyes were as sharp and wise as ever. He'd be thirty-three now. The same age as Frank and Jennifer.

Or rather, the same age Frank and Jennifer would be if they were still here.

"There are things we need to discuss." He returned his attention to her. "Some loose ends need tying up, but they can wait, if you'll set aside time for us to talk?"

"Of course."

Her focus darted over him—his broad shoulders, solid chest, lean hips and muscular legs. Every bit of his masculine stature was as imposing as her parents' sprawling estate at her back but infinitely warmer and more welcoming. It was a familiar feeling he'd always conjured up deep in her middle that she'd stifled long ago and had not expected to resurface today of all days. If anything, she'd expected him to be polite but resentful of her long-standing absence.

A choice she resented herself for making and hoped to rectify over time.

"Sophia's inside," he said. The small smile vanished. His lips firmed. "She's six months old now."

And you haven't bothered to visit her.

Face burning, Katie closed her eyes. He did resent her. The words might not be there, but the tone was. "I know. Jennifer emailed me pictures and we videoconferenced every week. Sophia's beautiful. Of course, she would be. I'm glad she and Emma inherited Jennifer's curls."

Landon's pensive gaze traveled over her hair, followed the length of it past her collarbone, lower, then snapped back to meet her eyes. He cleared his throat. "Yours, too."

"No." She picked at a curl. "These are courtesy of hot irons and hair spray. Mine's as straight as a stick, normally. Nothing like Jennifer's."

And that wasn't the only difference. All her life, her mother had pointed out the other ones on a routine basis and for years Katie had tried her best to mimic Jennifer's best qualities, though none of her attempts had ever met with her mother's approval.

Tires crunched over gravel and the sound of approaching footfalls mingled with that of an engine.

"Finally."

Katie tensed. There was no mistaking that brisk voice and cool tone. Reluctantly, she pulled her attention away from the sympathetic light in Landon's eyes and faced the source.

Her mother hadn't changed much, either. Clad in a pink blouse and formal pantsuit, Patricia stood beside the black limousine that had just arrived. Her brown eyes were already sizing her up and judging. And she sported the same staid demeanor along with a classy topknot, flawless makeup and high-end jewelry.

But...her fingers, balled around a crumpled tissue, shook slightly, and the necklace resting at the base of her throat jerked as her throat moved on a hard swallow.

Katie walked over and embraced her. "I'm sorry, Mom," she whispered against her perfumed neck. "I'm so sorry."

Her shoulders shook. She patted Katie on the back twice with one hand then drew away. "Had you arrived sooner, we would've had time for pleasantries but as it is, we're late." One eyebrow lifted as she studied Katie from head to toe. She leaned close and whispered, "Leather pants to your sister's funeral? What were you thinking, Katie?"

"Not much of anything," she said, clenching her teeth and blinking back tears.

It had hurt too much to think about what had happened to Jennifer and Frank. She'd been too afraid to imagine what their final moments had been like, how Matthew and Emma had felt after hearing the news or what a future without parents held for them. Instead, she'd gotten off the phone with her mother, bought a plane ticket, rented a car and called her boss to let her know she'd return in a week or two. She'd concentrated on the rugged peaks of the Smoky Mountains as the plane had descended then followed the curving yellow and white lines on the pavement as she'd driven the rest of the way to Elk Valley. Nothing had mattered other than getting to Matthew, Emma and Sophia as soon as possible.

It was only after she'd arrived, her composure finally breaking down in the car and her palms rubbing repetitively across the material covering her thighs, that she'd realized she had put on the same pants Jennifer had mailed to her for Christmas three years ago.

For the Sunset Strip, Jennifer had said over the phone, laughing. *I ordered them online. Wear them to The Viper Room and send me pics. Mom will have a hissy!*

"I like your pants, Aunt Katie."

A small hand patted her knee and she looked down. Emma, eyes sad and cheeks wet, blinked up at her.

"Oh, Emma." Katie sat on her haunches and wiped away one of Emma's tears with her thumb. She had Jennifer's creamy complexion and long lashes and had grown at least two inches in the months since she last saw her. "Thank you."

At a loss for more words, she tugged Emma forward and hugged her tight. The little girl's warm palms curled around her nape and the scent of fabric softener—Jennifer's favorite—wafted up from her black dress.

It was like hugging a little piece of Jennifer even after her sister had well and truly left her behind for good.

Katie squeezed Emma closer, imagining all the big moments in Emma's life Jennifer would miss and how painful life would be at times for Emma without her mother's support. Her heart broke all over again.

Emma shifted against her chest, her lips brushing Katie's ear. "You want me to hold your hand? Uncle Landon said it won't hurt as much if I do."

Uncle Landon? Katie glanced up at him. Jennifer had told her the kids spent a lot of time at Landon's ranch. That he was as good with them as Frank. Obviously, he was as much a fixture in the kids' lives as he'd been in hers and Jennifer's.

Landon smiled stiffly, dragged a hand over his face and walked toward the limo.

"I'd love that." Katie kissed Emma's cheek then stood.

Immediately, Emma slipped her hands in hers. Katie summoned up a smile as her dad walked over, Sophia cradled against his side.

"I'm glad you came home, Katydid." He kissed her forehead, hugging her close with his free arm.

Chest aching at the sorrow in his voice, Katie forced a laugh. "I'm too old for that nickname, but it's great to see you, too."

"You'll never be too old for it." His green eyes clouded with pain. "You'll always be my little girl no matter how old you get."

Katie smoothed a hand over Sophia's back. She was sound asleep and as precious in person as she'd been in her pictures. "Hi, beautiful."

A fresh wave of guilt rolled through her at having missed Sophia's birth. She should've come home long before now despite family tensions.

Frowning, Katie glanced around. "Where's Matthew?"

"Over here," Landon called.

Katie looked back at the limo. Matthew stood by Landon's side, mouth tightly set and eyes glaring. His lanky ten-year-old frame was stiff, his hands balled into fists at his sides.

"Hi, Matthew." Katie took a hesitant step forward. "I've missed you."

His dark eyes flashed—grief, anger and pain warring within—then he turned and slid inside the limo without saying a word.

Landon leaned inside, his voice muffled as he spoke to Matthew, then straightened and shook his head at Katie. "We'd better get on the road. The sooner we get this over with, the better."

Katie nodded, straining for another glimpse of Matthew. She curled her fingers tighter around Emma's hand, wondering how many pieces the kids' hearts would be in at the end of the day. Would it even be possible to put them back together again?

Two hours later, Katie stood by two coffins in Elk Valley Cemetery, holding back tears as mourners lined up, gave their condolences then returned to their cars. Some people she remembered, some she didn't. She stared at the roses adorning the caskets, their blooms full and bright beneath the late-afternoon sun, then looked at Matthew and Emma who stood nearby, staring silently at the ground.

True to her word, Emma had held her hand throughout the service then released it during the final prayer to wrap her arms around Landon's leg instead. Landon's strong shoulders had begun to sag and his eyes were tired. He'd cradled Sophia against his chest with one brawny arm the entire service, walking to the limo once to console her when she'd woken restless and grumpy, then returned with her sleeping in his arms.

"Landon." Katie touched his shoulder. "Would you like me to hold Sophia for a while?"

He turned away briefly to shake the last mourner's hand and thank her for her well-wishes then shook his head. "We need to head home soon. It'd be best not to disturb her this close to leaving."

Her heart sank just a bit more. She had no right to infringe on his bond with the kids, but her arms ached to comfort them.

"Okay," she whispered, glancing at her parents. They were both crying, obviously exhausted, and her mother had pulled away during each of her attempts to console her. All in all, home sounded like the better place to be right about now. "I could take Emma and Matthew back to the limo while you—"

"Katie Richards?" A man approached her, voice soft and hand outstretched. He tilted his head back to look up at her. She had a good six inches on him which, given her above-average height, was a common occurrence.

"Yes?"

"I'm Cecil Jenkins. Jennifer and Frank's lawyer," he said, extending his hand closer. "I wanted to tell you how sorry I am about your sister and brother-in-law. They were wonderful people."

Katie shook his hand. "Thank you."

"I know this must be a difficult time for you, but your sister secured my services three years ago and insisted that I give this to you in the event that..." He shrugged awkwardly. A blush stained his cheeks and spread over his bald head as he retrieved a white envelope from his jacket pocket.

"Cecil, this isn't the right time." Voice hard, Landon shifted Sophia to his other side. "Can't this wait until later?"

"I agree." Her mother, eyes red, moved to Landon's side and shook her head. "You're not to do this now."

Katie frowned. "What's going on?"

Cecil held up a hand. "Forgive me, but this isn't up to you, Patricia. Or any of us, for that matter. Jennifer and Frank were thorough in their wishes and this was part of their instructions. I'm legally bound to deliver this letter just as Jennifer requested."

Katie took the envelope, the pristine paper smooth beneath her fingertips. There were no markings other than her name. It was written in Jennifer's hand with an elegant flourish and a small heart dotting the *i*.

"It's time we get the children home." Patricia placed a hand on Matthew's shoulder, steering him toward the limo. "Let's go, Harold."

Her father nodded, took Emma's hand then followed.

Katie stared at the envelope, her fingertip tracing the curves of her name.

"Are you coming?" Landon half turned several feet away and peered at her over his shoulder. "We'll go back to your mom's, get the kids settled then talk."

"I..." Her hand tightened around the envelope and

an urgent need to see more of Jennifer's familiar hand-writing moved through her. "I'd like to read this now, if we can spare the time?"

Brow furrowing, Landon glanced down at Sophia, who still slept in his arms. "The kids really need some rest."

"I'd be happy to give Katie a ride back." Cecil smiled at her. "If you'd grant me the privilege?"

Katie nodded. "I'd appreciate that."

Cecil left to wait for her in his car and Katie watched as Landon settled Sophia inside the limo, cast her one last look then got inside, too. She waited until the limo rounded the cemetery's driveway then drove out of sight.

Hands shaking, she eased her fingernail underneath the lip of the envelope and carefully retrieved the letter. It was handwritten, just as she'd hoped. Warmth pulsed through her chest at the sight of the familiar script.

You're going to laugh, Katie. I know you will.

If I'm right, decades from now, when we're old and gray and living next door to each other with five cats like we planned, you'll find this letter and tease me with it and I'll regret ever having written it. But for now, I'll just say that Frank talked me into drawing up a will. Matthew is seven now, Emma just turned two and someday soon, we hope to have one more baby. I'm hoping for a pretty, passionate little girl that'll give us a run for our money. Someone like you. Which brings me to the reason I'm writing.

If I'm wrong, one day you'll read this and I

won't be with you. If this is the case, I'm sorry,
Katie. Sorrier than I could ever say.

The words blurred. Katie blinked hard and hot tears
rolled down her cheeks.

I don't know why things turn out the way they
do sometimes and I have no idea how old my children will be or what they'll be facing. What I do
know is that I want them to be raised by the person I admire most in the world. You.

Katie jerked her head up, stared at the empty stretch
of road the limo had just traveled, then spun around and
looked at the caskets. The breeze picked up, scattering
red petals across the dark wood.

So here it is: Matthew can be prideful and stubborn. He'll need your heart. Emma tends to be timid
and too trusting. She'll need your strength and dis-
cerning eye. And if Frank and I are lucky, you'll
have one more niece or nephew to get to know.
Frank has chosen Landon as secondary guardian, which means you'll have a partner in this,
and he'll be an excellent help if you need it. He's
a wonderful man and loves our kids as much as if
they were his own. Please give him as much time
with the kids as you can. And spend time with
him, too. I think you'll grow to trust and respect
him as much as Frank and I do. Landon will step
in if…for whatever reason, you're unable to follow
through. But I hope that's not the case.

Will you do it? For me? Because you love me? And because I've never loved another soul walking this earth more than I've loved you? I understand if you can't, but I hope you will. Because no matter how sad or afraid you might be, I promise you things will work out. My kids will love you as much I do and you'll love them, too. You'll help them laugh again, Katie. And you'll teach them how to live life to the fullest. I know you will. So, please do it for me.

And if you're second-guessing yourself, well… buck up, Katydid. Because there's nothing you can't handle.

Chapter 2

Landon believed a peaceful evening in east Tennessee could heal any wound afflicting a damaged soul. Tonight, however, proved there might be one he'd underestimated.

Using the edge of a side table, he cracked the cap off a cold beer, took a big swig then eased back in a rocking chair. He gazed into the distance, rocking slowly on the front porch of his home, and tried to find solace in familiar surroundings.

The moon, bright and full, nestled between two mountain peaks on the horizon, easing higher into the starlit sky and casting a white glow over the fifty-three acres of his small ranch. Rhythmic hoots of a barred owl, the rustle of small critters scampering in nearby woods and a snazzy chorus of katydids were tonight's song.

A low sound escaped Landon's lips—half laugh, half harrumph. "Katydid."

Rascal, a middle-aged German shepherd, rose from his relaxed pose on the porch floor and perked his ears. He stuck one large paw out, settling it beside the toe of Landon's boot.

"Sorry, bud." Landon forced a smile and patted his thick fur. "Go back to sleep."

He lowered back to his belly, nuzzled his black nose against Landon's leg and closed his eyes.

Landon took a heftier swig of his beer then rolled the fizzy beverage over his tongue. Jennifer's nickname for Katie had taken hold when they were kids and she'd often used it to give Katie an extra push whenever she'd been scared or nervous.

Katydids can thrive anywhere, she'd once told Katie.

Several years ago, he'd accompanied Jennifer and Frank, who'd recently married, to Elk Valley's spring festival to cheer Katie on in the talent show. She'd been eighteen, terrified and refused to step onto the stage into the spotlight. A little prodding from Jennifer, though, and Katie had stridden out there and belted out a lonely tune sweet enough to moisten most eyes in hearing range, including his own.

She'd won a trophy and, if he were a betting man, he'd wager she'd won a whole lot of hearts, too. The question now was, after receiving word of Jennifer's wishes, would Katie try to win her sister's children, too?

No telling what was in that letter or where Katie was at the moment. He'd waited at Patricia's house for hours, comforting the kids and hoping Katie would return, express her astonishment at the discovery and immediately ask to relinquish her rights. Only, she hadn't shown. So he'd given up, kissed the kids good-night then left them with Patricia, at her request, for the evening.

For all he knew, instead of being tempted to give in to Jennifer's wishes, Katie may have done exactly as Patricia had predicted and hauled ass the moment she finished reading the letter. Which wouldn't bode well for the kids having any decent kind of relationship with her.

Or she could be in Cecil's office right now, demanding every detail of primary guardianship, then assume the role while he sat here and chugged beer.

Quite frankly, he didn't know which scenario was worse.

He closed his eyes and rolled his head against the chair's headrest. The heavy weight of grief lodged in his throat and pressed hard on his ribs. Man, he didn't want to think about it. Fact was, he didn't want to think about anything beyond keeping the pain at bay and helping the kids pack their belongings tomorrow morning.

Moving them into his home and getting them settled on the ranch was priority one. To the point that he'd have to grieve for Frank and Jennifer later. Much later. After he helped the kids through their own period of mourning.

Emma hadn't worried him as much. She'd fought with a brave face throughout the service like a trouper. And Sophia was too young to fully conceive of the loss as of yet. Matthew, on the other hand—

The owl screeched in the distance, a furious flap of wings followed, then the growl of an engine flooded the valley, echoing off the surrounding mountain range.

A car roared down the curvy driveway then jerked to a halt amid a thick cloud of dust.

Rascal sprang up, barking.

"Ah, hell." Landon jumped to his feet and grabbed his collar gently. "Easy, Rascal."

The driver's-side door slammed and Katie's slim figure worked its way quickly up the graveled walkway in the dark.

"Is this what you wanted to talk to me about before I left?" Paper crinkled and a shapely arm waved something white that caught the moonlight. "What was it you called them? Loose ends?"

"Nice to see you again, Katie," he called out. "Wished you woulda called first and let me know you were coming."

She stopped, her high heels thudding on the bottom porch step, and looked up at him. The moonlight bathed the curve of her flushed cheek and her chin trembled.

"I'm sorry," she whispered. "I didn't mean to intrude or be so crass." She shoved her long hair over her shoulders and moved closer, bringing her hurt-filled eyes into view. "I just can't believe this—any of it. I spoke to Cecil. He took me to his office and I read the will. He said you knew, that my mom knew, too. And neither one of you bothered to tell me."

His face heated. "I didn't know how to tell you. I've never dealt with anything like this before and I was waiting for the right time."

"When?" A pained look crossed her face. "After I left again? Because that's what both of you thought I'd do, right? Just dump the kids on you and walk away as though Matthew, Emma and Sophia are just—" she shook her head "—loose ends?"

Landon set down his beer then shifted from one foot to the other. Her words hit closer to the truth than he wanted to admit.

"Do the kids know?" she asked.

"No. I thought it'd be best if we discussed things first." He nudged Rascal to the side, commanded him to stay put then opened the front door. "Please come in. I'll get you a drink then we'll sit down and talk."

She hovered, those beautiful eyes of hers moving from him to Rascal then back. She sighed then ascended the steps, a barely audible *"thank you"* preceding her.

Landon led the way through the small living room to the even smaller kitchen then waited on the threshold for her to join him. She'd stopped in the living room and her head turned slowly as she studied the scuffed hardwood floors, low ceilings and sparse furniture. Craning her neck to the side, she studied the empty hallway.

"You still here on your own?" she asked. "Jennifer never mentioned you having a girlfriend or getting married." Panic flashed across her pretty features as she thrust her hand, palm down, toward the floor. "Just so we're clear, I'm not involved in any of Jennifer's starry-eyed matchmaking tricks. I'm perfectly happy on my own and won't be moving back to Elk Valley. So if that talk you keep suggesting we have could possibly include Jennifer's idea of marriage as a solution to this predicament, please know it was never my idea and I have no intention of ever coercing you into anything along those lines."

A rueful laugh escaped him. "As blunt as ever, I see."

She had the good grace to wince. "Sorry. I've never had a filter. And I didn't mean to imply you wouldn't be good husband material. Or that I don't find you attract—" A squeak escaped her parted lips. "I mean... that other women wouldn't find you attractive...or want to marry y—" Her eyes closed. "Oh, Lord."

Stifling a smile, he shook his head. "It's just me."

Until tomorrow. Then the kids would move in and brighten the dark loneliness of this empty house.

So far, the worn couch, rickety recliner and small TV had suited him just fine. Though all of it was a far cry from the affluent surroundings Katie had grown up in at Patricia's and probably subpar to her current lifestyle in California. He hated to admit it, but this place probably looked like a hovel compared to hers.

His cheeks flamed. "I've ordered a new love seat and sofa," he said, rocking back on his heels. "They'll be here later this week."

She faced him, her thoughtful gaze piercing his calm facade, making his skin prickle. "For the kids?"

He nodded. "Patricia and Harold are helping me move Matthew's and Emma's beds in first thing tomorrow morning. Sophia's crib is already set up in one bedroom and I just finished clearing out two more for Emma and Matthew."

"Everything's all planned, huh?" Her posture stiffened, her low words almost an aside. "The secondary guardian steps in and my nieces and nephew pack up and head to your ranch."

"I'm not upper class, Katie," he said. "But I promise you they won't want for anything."

Katie studied him closer, her intense gaze still picking his thoughts apart, and then whispered, "Do you think I'm angry with you? That I'm judging you?"

He shoved his hands in his pockets, a wry smile twisting his lips. "I'm kinda picking up on that, yeah."

Her shoulders slumped. She released a ragged breath then crossed the room to his side.

Landon fixed his eyes straight ahead, focused on the framed picture on the wall across the room rather than the soft brush of Katie's hair against his biceps. Frank, dressed in graduation regalia, smiled back at him, one of his arms around Jennifer, the other propped on Landon's shoulder.

"I am angry." Katie's voice softened. "But not with you. I was hurt when I found out you hadn't told me about the will…" Her hand wrapped around his wrist, the soft pads of her fingers skimming over his forearm along the way. "That's not fair to you, I know. I haven't kept in touch or been the kind of friend to you that Frank or Jennifer was and I know I didn't deserve it. But it's how I felt."

He inclined his head, her light touch and gentle tone easing the tension in his limbs.

"I'm angry with myself for not being here for the kids," she added. "For Jennifer and Frank." She leaned in and her soft breath tickled his neck. "And for you. I know you're hurting and that you miss them. I know you love the kids and that you're doing what you think is best. You always do."

Her touch was an innocent gesture meant to comfort and console, but an undercurrent—one that had existed between them for years—accompanied the action. One that had always weakened his defenses and made him long for more than friendship from her in the past.

He faced her then, and she looked up at him, her brown eyes full of regret, grief and uncertainty. He'd felt the same painful emotions since losing Frank and Jennifer, and it was a small, if somewhat selfish, relief to know he wasn't alone. Aching to comfort her in return, he tugged his hands from his pockets and cupped her jaw.

"Have you ever been afraid of anything, Landon?" She placed her warm palms on his chest. Her fingertips curled into his thin T-shirt, the gentle pressure making his body hum. "Even once? Even if it was something small?"

The uncertain tremor in her voice coaxed him closer. Remaining silent, he smoothed his thumb over her tempting bottom lip, the urge to fling responsibility over his shoulder, lower his head and touch his mouth to hers almost overwhelming.

"Jennifer told me she thought you were too strong to know what fear was." She stared at his mouth, the nervous tension and heat in her darkening eyes almost tangible, then pulled back and walked away. "Sometimes, I believe that."

Realizing his hands still hung motionless in the air, he shoved them back in his pockets and straightened.

"What she's asked of me..." Katie stood at the front door, her back to him. "It scares me so much. Matthew, Emma and Sophia deserve someone better equipped for this than I am."

Words clamored up his throat, tangled on his tongue and prodded his mouth open. He wanted to offer her reassurance. But the truth was, she wasn't responsible or dependable enough to be a good parent for the kids, no matter how much Jennifer may have believed otherwise. And no matter how much he wanted to believe otherwise now.

"I really am sorry I barged in on you like this, especially when you have an early day ahead tomorrow." She glanced over her shoulder as she opened the door. "I let my temper get ahold of me as usual. It was rude and insensitive. Contrary to popular belief, I'm better than that and hope you won't hold it against me."

Rascal scampered in from the porch then nudged Katie's thigh with his nose.

Smiling, she squatted beside him and scratched behind his ear. "What's his name?"

Landon rubbed the painful throb in his temple. "Rascal."

"Rascal," she repeated, giggling as he licked her chin. "I bet Landon takes good care of you, yeah?" She kissed the top of Rascal's head then stood, saying quietly, "He takes good care of everyone."

"Come by in the morning. Help me move the kids in?" Landon stifled a groan. Damn, he wished he'd had the good sense not to extend the invitation—but too late now. "It'd give you a chance to spend some time with them before you leave."

"Before I leave?" She cocked her head to the side. A new gleam, steady and defiant, brightened her eyes. "Do you think that's what I should do? Sign my nieces and nephew over to you then take off?"

"I didn't say that." *But I hope like hell that's what you'll do.* Somehow, Katie's impulsive nature always managed to complicate everything. "We're starting around eight after I finish morning chores. Get here a little earlier and I'll get you that drink I promised."

Her lips quirked and she poked her head outside to glance at the bottle he'd left on the porch. "Coffee or beer?"

He grinned. "Which eases that temper of yours better?"

"Coffee," she stated matter-of-factly then smiled at him, her expression softening. "Sweet and strong."

His blood rushed hotly through his veins and his abs tightened. Every nerve ending in his body tingled at her innocent words and he ached to reach out, enfold her in his arms and kiss her in the sweetest, strongest way her tone suggested.

But…this attraction he had for her was nothing new, and more unwelcome than ever considering the circumstances.

"I'll have it ready." He cleared the husky feeling from his throat, escorted her to the front porch then watched as she walked to her car. "Be careful on the way out," he called. "There are ruts in the road so you might want to take it slow."

Katie didn't answer. Just flashed a bigger smile, slid in the driver's seat then sped away.

Clouds of dust drifted across the moonlit valley after she departed, the routine throb of nocturnal creatures resumed and Rascal rejoined him on the porch. Everything was back in its proper place and peacefully predictable…until she returned in the morning.

Have you ever been afraid of anything, Landon?

He flexed his hands. The silky feel of Katie's creamy

skin still lingered on his palms and despite his best ef-
fort to ignore it, a small corner of his heart wondered if
she'd changed over the years. If maybe this time, given
the circumstances and Jennifer's prodding, Katie might
actually put someone else's needs before her own. If she
might try to be a better aunt to the kids, and possibly a
better friend to him. Or maybe even something more?

The thought of leaving himself vulnerable to Katie's whims stirred an uncomfortable churn in his gut.
He sat back down in his chair and reminded himself of
exactly how much he had to lose.

"What do you want to do?"

Katie bit her fingernail, wincing when she hit the
quick, then pressed a button on the steering wheel to
increase the volume of the call coming through the
speakers. "That's the problem. I don't know. I mean I
do know, but…"

Sandra Martin, Katie's best friend and most recent
marketing client, hummed thoughtfully over the line.
"It would change everything. Your entire life as you
know it. You'd have to get a bigger apartment, change
your work hours *and* diapers, choose a pediatrician, attend PTA meetings, stay home nights and weekends,
and all that's just scratching the surface. Not to mention the increase in financial burdens. There are very
real, very big challenges to think about with this type
of commitment."

Katie sighed. "I know."

She kneaded the kink in the back of her neck—Elk
Valley Motel's lumpy beds and a 5:00 a.m. wake-up
call did absolutely no favors for anyone—then navi-

gated a sharp curve as she descended a mountain toward Landon's ranch.

"Big," Sandra repeated, a smile in her voice. "Real big. As in, you'd have to learn how to make something for breakfast other than toast or cereal."

Katie laughed. "Hey, no one knows how to butter a piece of burned toast like me."

Sandra was silent for a moment then said, "We're laughing now but think about how your days will be if you take this on. You know I'll support you whatever your choice ends up being, but in the end it'll be you, a ten-year-old, five-year-old and six-month-old. In California. Alone. That would be your new reality."

The graveled driveway leading to Landon's ranch emerged into view.

Katie bit the inside of her cheek and slowed the car. "But if I walk away…how would that make them feel? They'll think I've abandoned them. What kind of aunt or sister does that? What kind of person would that make me?"

"The kind who chose a different path years ago." Sandra's tone gentled. "Settling down in Elk Valley and having children was Jennifer's dream, not yours. You're entitled to live the life you've built, and you can still see the kids and support them. Just as an aunt—not a mom. There's nothing wrong with wanting something different out of life." An indrawn breath whispered over the line. "You've spoken a lot about the kids, but you haven't told me much about this Landon character. What's he like?"

Sweet. Strong. And sexier than he'd ever been. Katie rolled her lips together before those last thoughts slipped out. It wouldn't do to say them out loud. It was bad enough that she was thinking and feeling them. "He's patient and intelligent," she said matter-of-factly. "He's honest, dependable, hardworking—"

"And a good guy?" Sandra asked. "I mean, if you decide not to take this on, he's the one they'll end up with, right?"

"Yeah." Katie pulled to stop beside Landon's truck, her chest warming as she caught sight of him leading a horse into the large barn. Rascal followed his every step. "He's definitely a good guy. And he'd probably be a perfect parent."

Which made her feel like an even bigger heel. Here she was, blood kin, debating whether or not to take responsibility for her nieces and nephew whereas Landon, who had no biological relation to the kids, hadn't hesitated to welcome them into his life.

"Look, can I call you back later tonight?" Katie rubbed her temples. "I really need to go but I promise none of this will interfere with our plans. I don't want you to worry about your account, okay? I'm on top of it. When I finish here, I'm going back to the motel and drawing up the best marketing strategy on the planet. Sexy Suds will be in every bath boutique in the nation by the time I'm done."

"Oh, I'm not worried. You're the best there is. I just want you to take some time for yourself and think things over before you make a decision. Remember I'm here for you no matter what, okay?"

"Thanks, Sandra."

Katie cut the engine, then headed up the trail toward the barn. The morning sun rose above the green mountaintops and spilled over the rolling hills below. Large hay bales dotted the emerald fields, white flowers lined the length of the pasture fence and the scent of honeysuckle sweetened the fresh air.

"Same as you remember?" Landon reemerged from the barn. He took long strides down the dirt path in her direction, his jeans pulling snug across his thick thighs with each step while Rascal pranced at his side. "It's been a long time since you've visited Elk Valley in the spring."

Katie took another long look around as he drew near. Two ranch hands walked across the pasture, leading horses toward the barn.

"It's as beautiful as always," she said. "Especially here. Are you still boarding horses?"

"Yeah." His blond hair gleamed in the sunlight. "We have fifteen at the moment and will start riding lessons soon." He gestured toward the house. "Wanna come in? Coffee's waiting, as promised."

"Thank you."

She followed him inside to the kitchen, sat on a bar stool at the small island and watched the strong muscles of his back ripple beneath his T-shirt as he retrieved two mugs from the cabinet.

"I'd like to apologize again for last night," she said. "I really didn't mean to spring in on you like that."

"It's okay." He lifted a mug toward her. "Strong and sweet, right? No cream?"

"Yes, please."

The rich aroma of coffee filled the kitchen as he poured them both a mug then added sugar to each. She took the mug he offered, drank a small sip then hummed with approval. Rascal padded to her side and sat.

Reaching down, she rubbed behind his ear and tried to still her racked nerves. "How many rooms are we setting up today?"

"Two." Landon set his mug down on a coaster, slipped one beneath her mug then leaned onto his muscular forearms across from her. "Emma's and Matthew's."

"And how many bedrooms do you have in all?"

"Five."

"Bathrooms?"

"Two." He frowned. "Am I being interrogated for a reason here?"

"No. Sorry." Neck tingling, she took another sip of coffee. "I'm just curious about the arrangements. I think I gave you the idea that I was unimpressed with your home last night and that wasn't the case at all. You have a beautiful place and my apartment is a fraction of the size of your house. If the kids come home with me, I'll barely have…"

His blue eyes hardened and a muscle ticked in his jaw as he stared.

Her face heated.

"It's not my place to tell you what decision to make," he said softly, "and I certainly don't want you to think I'm trying to overstep here, but I love those kids as much as you do and what they need most right now is stability."

"I know." She wrapped her palms tighter around the mug and focused on the heat singeing her palms rather than the hollow in her chest. "I want that for them, too," she said, though she'd spent the majority of a sleepless night conceding it would be difficult for her to provide stability without making the major changes Sandra had mentioned earlier. It was an intimidating thought that clashed with her desire to abide by Jennifer's wishes.

"Your mom mentioned you'd gone into marketing." Landon's long finger tapped the rim of his coffee mug. "Where are you working these days?"

"KC Marketing in Los Angeles," she said. "I'm a brand manager."

"For lingerie and alcoholic beverages of all things," Patricia said.

Katie glanced over her shoulder. Her mother stood in the kitchen doorway, a large diaper bag draped over one shoulder, Sophia in her arms and one eyebrow lifted in disapproval.

"Once," Katie said. "For both. I managed one account for a good friend who opened a San Leandro brewery and another for my supervisor's cousin who happens to be one of the most promising talents in fashion right now. Both were great learning experiences."

Patricia pursed her lips. "And the account after those two? What was the name of it?"

Katie set her mug on the table. She licked her lips, fixed her gaze on the clock hanging on the wall behind her mother's left shoulder and whispered, "Passionate Pucker."

Patricia narrowed her eyes and tilted her head. "I'm sorry, what was that?"

Katie sighed then announced loudly, "I said, Passionate Pucker."

Landon straightened from his relaxed position on the other side of the island. A guarded expression crossed his face, but curiosity filled his blue eyes as he studied her mouth.

"Lip wear." Katie spread her hands and shrugged. "You know, balms, stains and glosses?" She faced her mother. "The name's just a marketing tactic, and I don't see why you have such a problem with what I do for a living."

"I don't have a problem with you being a brand manager," Patricia said. "I just wish you'd choose more wholesome, family-friendly brands. Though that's not a concern for you since you don't have children."

Katie tapped her heel against the stool leg. "I don't have children now, but—"

"I'm sorry for not knocking, Landon." Patricia smiled at him, effectively ending her debate with Katie. "The door was open and Matthew was anxious to get started. He's so excited about moving in with you."

Matthew walked in carrying a goldfish bowl. "Uncle Landon, can I leave Jinx in here while we set up the table?"

Matthew stopped, his eyes landing on Katie, and a dark flush crept across his face. There were dark shadows under his eyes and his hair was rumpled. The bright happiness she'd last seen in his eyes years ago was absent.

Katie slid off the bar stool and ran a clammy hand over her jeans. "Hey, Matthew." She gestured toward Landon. "I was invited to help move your things in today. I hope that's okay?"

Matthew looked at Landon and Patricia then lowered his head and stared at the fishbowl in his hands.

"Do you have a bigger tank for—what was his name?" she asked. "Jinx?"

He nodded but didn't look up.

"I could help you set it up, if you'd like me to? Then I could take you all out for dinner tonight at the motel. My treat."

He walked across the room, set the bowl on the counter and watched Jinx swim two laps around the bowl before saying, "I guess. Emma's bringing in the plastic trees and stuff. The tank's in Grandpa's truck. It's heavy."

"I'll grab it," Landon said, rounding the island. "Matthew, why don't you show Katie to your new room? You'll need to pick out where you want to put it first."

After Landon left, Matthew trudged out of the kitchen and Katie followed him to the hallway.

"Katie?"

She watched as Matthew entered a bedroom at the end of the hall and said, "I'll be there in a minute, Matthew," then glanced over her shoulder at her mother.

"How long do you plan to stay this time?" Patricia asked.

That all-too-familiar ache seeped back into Katie's chest. "I'm not sure," she said quietly. "Why? You anxious for me to leave?"

Patricia sighed. "Whether you believe it or not, we have missed you."

"I know. I've missed all of you, too." Katie looked at Sophia, who blinked wide brown eyes up at her. "Would you mind if I hold Sophia for a while? Just until Landon gets the aquarium inside?"

Patricia hesitated and glanced at Sophia before nodding reluctantly. "I suppose. In the meantime, I'll help Harold bring in the kids' bags."

Katie walked over, took Sophia then settled her on her hip. Sophia balled her fists in Katie's shirt, smiled up at her and squealed. She had dimples—tiny indentations on each side of her mouth in exactly the same place Jennifer's had been.

"Hi, precious." Katie's eyes blurred and she blinked rapidly as Sophia bounced in her arms. "You're raring to go this morning, aren't you?"

"She had a good night's sleep." Patricia sniffed and bit her lip.

Katie swallowed hard. "She looks so much like Jennifer, doesn't she?"

"And you." Patricia wiped a lone tear from her cheek then headed for the door. "She looks like you, Katie."

It was quiet after she left. Katie cuddled Sophia closer and studied the shape of the baby's eyes, her pug nose, rosebud mouth and brown curls.

"You definitely have your mama's hair," Katie said, smiling. "But I think my mom's right. You might have gotten a little piece of me, as well."

Sophia gurgled and reached up, the tiny fingers of one hand winding in Katie's bangs and the other curling around her earlobe. Katie dipped her head, inviting Sophia to explore further. Sophia patted Katie's cheeks, hiccupped then grinned.

Katie laughed. Sophia's comforting weight in her arms warmed her heart and eased some of the pain.

You'll help them laugh again, Katie. I know you will. So, please do it for me.

She stilled as Jennifer's plea whispered in her mind. It left an odd mixture of excitement and fear in its wake.

"What kind of aunt would I be," she whispered, slipping her pointer finger into Sophia's tight grip and starting toward Matthew's bedroom, "if I left you all behind?"

There was movement across the room. Landon stood on the other side of the island, his muscular arms weighed down with a large aquarium stand. His eyes focused on Sophia then drifted up to Katie, and the same fear Katie harbored was reflected in his disapproving gaze.

Chapter 3

Katie twisted a paper napkin tighter around her finger as she looked out the window of the Elk Valley Motel restaurant. The dim lights in the parking lot barely reached the group ambling toward the side entrance of the restaurant, but she could just make out the exhausted droop of Matthew's expression in the darkness.

"Oh, Jennifer," she whispered. "What were you thinking, asking me to do this?"

Katie didn't have much experience with kids. As a teen, she'd only babysat twice for close friends of her parents, but she supposed she could take comfort in the fact that she didn't recall any disasters occurring, which meant she must've done something right. Even so, her afternoon with Matthew at Landon's ranch hadn't gone as great as she'd hoped.

After unloading bed frames and mattresses then maneuvering furniture into the kids' new bedrooms, Katie had spent the better part of the afternoon helping Emma and Matthew unpack their bags, hang clothes in their small closets and tuck fresh sheets on their beds. She and Matthew had set up the aquarium in relative silence, considering he'd only responded to her attempts at conversation with close-ended one-word responses. It hadn't helped that her cell phone had buzzed every ten minutes with questions from her boss who wanted updates on Sandra's Sexy Suds account as well as two potential new accounts.

Around five, she'd excused herself and returned to her motel room, answered work emails and showered and changed for dinner. Then she'd taken up residence at a corner table in the restaurant, sipped lemonade and fidgeted while she waited for Landon and the kids to arrive.

"Have a nice dinner, invite them for a picnic tomorrow then say good-night—not goodbye." She moved closer to the window, watching Landon lead Emma and Matthew up the walkway. "No matter what happens, make sure they know this won't be goodbye."

"Are you okay, hon?"

Katie jerked away from the window and nodded at the concerned waitress hovering by the table.

"Yes, thank you." She smiled apologetically, recognizing the woman's familiar features but unable to pair a name with them. "I'm just talking to myself like an idiot."

And trying to choke back the tenth round of tears for the day.

The waitress eyed the twisted remnants of napkins littering the table then grinned. "Nervous about something?"

Oh, just praying for forgiveness from my sister for not honoring her wishes and figuring out how to prove to her children that I love them even though I'll board a plane and fly back to California without them next week.

"A bit, yeah."

"Anything I can do to help?"

Katie shook her head and motioned toward the entrance. "Thank you, but the people I'm meeting are here and—"

The bell over the door chimed. Emma and Matthew walked in then Landon followed with Sophia perched on his hip.

"Landon Eason!" The waitress clapped her hands together and smiled. "Feels like ages since I've seen you."

He smiled back. "Nina. Good to see you."

Nina Griffin. That was it. She was the mother of one of Frank's high school friends and Katie recalled seeing her at Friday night football games years ago. It wasn't surprising that Nina didn't recognize her. Katie had always been overshadowed by her sister in Elk Valley. Since leaving, Katie had worked hard to reinvent herself. California was where she'd found a home and achieved the success she'd craved.

Nina's tone softened as Landon approached. "I was so sorry to hear about Frank and Jennifer."

Landon nodded then smoothed a hand over Emma's hair. "Thought we'd stop by for a bite to eat."

Nina glanced down at Matthew and Emma. "Well,

this is a wonderful surprise. I'd have thought you'd have dropped in on your sister instead."

Katie winced. Oh, no. She'd forgotten Amber, Landon's sister, owned a café in Elk Valley. All things considered, he probably thought she was an inconsiderate jerk to overlook his family's restaurant at a time like this.

She stepped forward. "I'm sorry, Landon. I totally forgot about Amber's café. If you'd like, we could—"

He held up a hand. "No, this is fine. We haven't been here in a while and—" he winked "—Nina's great company."

"Oh, you sweet flirt." Nina laughed. "Have a seat and get comfortable. I'll grab some more menus."

"Thanks." Landon nudged Emma toward the chair at Katie's side then rubbed Sophia's back. "We could use a high char if you have one, please?"

"Sure thing, hon."

Great. Just great. First she forgets about Amber's restaurant then didn't have the good sense to have a high char ready for Sophia.

Ducking her head, Katie hastily gathered up the twisted napkins and shoved them to the other side of the table. "Sorry, I should've taken care of that, too."

Unsurprised resignation gleamed in Landon's eyes. He thanked Nina when she returned with a high char, settled Sophia inside then sat by Matthew. Clean jeans stretched across his thick thighs as he situated his muscular frame on the thinly padded seat, the light spice of his cologne releasing with each of his movements.

Clearly, he'd taken time to freshen up, too. His gorgeous male frame, courteous demeanor and calm strength stirred every nerve ending in her body.

Resisting the urge to walk around the small table, wrap her arms around his lean waist and nuzzle against his broad chest, Katie sat beside Emma then smiled at the kids. "Thank you for joining me."

Emma paused chewing her gum and grinned up at her, eyes tired but kind. "You're welcome, Aunt Katie."

Sophia cooed and gummed her fist. Matthew frowned down at the table.

Katie leaned closer. "How does Jinx like his new surroundings?"

Matthew scoffed but didn't look up. "He's a fish. He's always in water."

"Yes, but he's in a new room now," Katie said. "And we put him in front of that big window overlooking Landon's ranch. I bet he's enjoying the view."

Matthew sat back in his seat and crossed his arms, his tone dry. "He's a fish. It's not like we have conversations and stuff."

"Well—" Katie tucked a curl behind her ear with a shaky hand "—when I was your age, your mom and I had two goldfish. One was really small. We named him Megalodon so he wouldn't get an inferiority complex. We talked to him all the time." Her throat thickened and she tried for a smile. "He never talked back, of course, but we gave it our best shot."

If possible, Matthew's expression darkened even more. "That's stupid."

"No, it's not." Emma's chin trembled. "Mama wasn't stupid and Aunt Katie can talk to Jinx as much as she wants."

Landon cleared his throat. "All right. It's been a long

day and we're all tired and cranky, so let's give the fish a rest and order, okay?"

Hands trembling, Katie gulped more lemonade.

Nina, bless her blissful heart, returned to the table with menus at the perfect time, leaving them to relax back in their seats and study the large laminated lists. They ordered and fifteen minutes later, their food arrived. Nina set plates of burgers and fries in front of Landon and the kids, a bowl of applesauce on Sophia's high char and a fruit salad at Katie's place setting.

"That's all you're eating?" Landon narrowed his eyes at the small pile of sliced strawberries, bananas, grapes and apricots.

"I drank about six glasses of lemonade before y'all got here so I'm pretty full already." And her stomach was twisting so much, it wouldn't be wise to try anything else at the moment. She glanced at Sophia. "Besides, I thought I'd share with Sophia. That is, if she's able to eat solids yet?"

Landon nodded, but waved away the offer. "She likes bananas but she's allergic to apricots. With it all mixed up like that, it's not safe to give her any."

"Oh." Katie squirmed. "I didn't know."

He shrugged then grabbed a napkin. "How could you?"

It wasn't the words he'd said so much as the tone of his voice.

A burning sensation crept over Katie's neck and chest. Of course she wouldn't know. Because to him, she was nothing more than an irresponsible stranger who knew nothing about her nieces and nephew.

The offhanded remark hovered over the table as

Landon tucked the napkin under Sophia's collar. He dipped a spoon in the applesauce then froze. His lean cheeks flushed a shade of red that had to feel as hot as her own.

He faced her, his blue eyes gentle as they met hers. "I'm sorry. I didn't mean it like that. I really didn't."

No, he hadn't. He was too polite and considerate to do such a thing, and the facts were facts no matter how much of a loser they made her feel like.

"I know." She stabbed a strawberry with her fork, chewed it twice then choked it down, hoping to smother the guilt roiling in her gut.

Landon sighed then tucked a spoonful of applesauce into Sophia's open mouth. She grinned and a happy sigh escaped her as she gummed the fruit.

"It's a shame I forgot about Amber's café," Katie murmured. "I bet Sophia loves your sister's banana pudding." She watched as Landon grabbed a napkin and wiped applesauce from Sophia's chin. "How's Amber doing, by the way? Jennifer told me…"

She glanced at Matthew. His frown deepened as he picked up his glass of sweet tea and sipped.

"I heard Amber married Nate Tenley," Katie continued.

"Yeah." Landon took a bite of his burger, chewed then said, "They're doing well. Nate asked me to watch the kids tomorrow so he and Amber can have a day out."

"They have kids?"

"Triplets. Two boys and one girl. They're two and a half now."

"Wow."

She'd been surprised at Jennifer's news that free-spirited bull rider Nate had finally settled down, and she'd been even more surprised that he'd decided to do so with his friend's sister, considering how overprotective Landon had always been of Amber. But Nate becoming a dad? Well, that was a shock.

"Three toddlers." Katie glanced around the table. "So, you'll be watching half a dozen kids at the ranch tomorrow?"

"No big deal. I'm used to babysitting. I've had lots of practice." Landon held a napkin out toward Emma then said, "Gum, sweetheart. You can't eat while you're chewing that."

"Yes, sir." Emma took out her gum then placed it in the napkin.

Katie nodded slowly, watching the deft movements of his long fingers and muscled forearms as he disposed of the gum then wiped Sophia's chin clean again. "Guess that's why you're so good with kids."

"It's because he's here all the time." Matthew slammed his glass onto the table. Ice and sweet tea splattered onto his plate and made a puddle between his fries and burger. "He likes kids. He likes *us.* So why don't you go ahead and leave?"

"Matthew." Voice curt, Landon shot him a disapproving look.

"I…" The look of anger and distrust on Matthew's face made Katie slump back in her chair. Dear God, there was hatred in his eyes. As though he couldn't stand the sight of her. "I like you, too, Matthew. All of you. That's why I'm here. I missed y—"

"No, you didn't." His face crumpled and tears spilled onto his lashes. "You only came back because Mama died. Because she asked you to take us. I don't want to go with you. I don't want you at all."

A lump lodged in her throat. Oh, she couldn't cry again. Not in front of the kids. "I do care about you."

"You care about your job." His chin trembled but he glared through the tears.

"Where'd you hear all this?" Landon asked quietly.

"Gammie. She told Grandpa last night that Aunt Katie wouldn't do it. That she'd leave next week." He shoved his chair back then stood and scowled at Katie. "You don't have to wait till then. Go ahead and leave now."

With that, Matthew got up from the table and ran across the restaurant to the front door then out into the parking lot.

Katie watched his small figure dart across the black asphalt and into the night, the sounds of Emma's sobs at her side making the guilt inside her grow.

"Are you really leaving, Aunt Katie?"

She looked down at Emma and tried to speak but nothing would come out.

Landon shoved to his feet. "I'm sorry, but we gotta go."

He removed the napkin from Sophia's collar then gently lifted her into his arms. She bobbed against his biceps, reaching for the applesauce and crying when she couldn't grab it.

Katie helped Emma down from her chair then stood, twisting her hands together against her middle as Landon hurried Emma toward the door. "Will you call me tonight so I know he's okay?"

Landon hesitated, glancing from her to the parking

lot and back again. "Yeah. I'll call you." He raised his voice over Sophia's increasing sobs and tugged Emma's arm. "Come on, sweetheart."

Emma quickened her step but looked over her shoulder, tears streaming down her cheeks. "Bye, Aunt Katie."

Katie stood motionless as they walked away. "Goodbye."

Landon sat on the living room floor, propped his forearms on his knees and frowned at the colorful chaos flashing across the TV. Why in the hell had he caved under the kids' pressure, changed his mind and allowed them to hook up that aggravating video game contraption? It was loud, distracting and looked completely out of place on his rustic wood entertainment stand.

He glanced to his left where Matthew sat, legs crossed, fingers springing from one knob to another on a controller. "Matthew?"

No response.

"I cut you some slack on the way home from the motel," he continued, "but I told you we were gonna talk tonight and it's that time."

Nothing. The kid didn't even blink.

"You want that thing to spend the night in the house or in the hayfield?"

That did it. Matthew sighed, dropped the controller then reached over and powered down the game console.

"I know you're angry with your aunt Katie, but—"

"I'm not angry."

Landon studied the hard clench of his jaw and dark circles under his eyes. "Well, you look angry." He softened his voice as he said, "And sad. Which you have every right to be."

Matthew turned away and fixed his gaze on the wall in front of him. "I don't want her here."

"Aunts aren't a dime a dozen, you know. They're pretty important people to have in your life."

"Good ones are," Matthew said tightly. "I already have Aunt Amber."

Landon nodded. "Amber's great—I'll give you that—but she's my sister, not your mother's. Other than your dad, your aunt Katie was closer to your mom than anyone else. I can tell you about your dad, but Katie has memories of your mom that'll help you know her better."

"They're both gone and they're never coming back." Matthew's voice cracked. "So, what does it matter?"

Landon looked away, a feeling way too similar to despair surging over him. "We're all hurting, Matthew. Katie, especially. There's no point in trying to hurt her more."

It'd taken everything he'd had to walk away from her two hours ago and chase Matthew. He'd kept seeing her face long after he'd driven the kids home. That wounded look in her eyes had stayed with him as he'd finished feeding Sophia. And when he'd put Sophia and Emma to bed, he hadn't been able to shake the image of how helpless Katie had looked standing in that restaurant as they'd left, her hands hanging heavy by her sides, drawing her usually proud shoulders down.

She'd looked so lost and vulnerable. So alone.

"Katie tried real hard to make things right today despite you shoving her back and claiming your space,"

Landon continued. "The least you could do is try to meet her halfway."

"She doesn't know us, she doesn't know what she's doing and she's never here anyway."

"She's here now, and I expect you to be civil."

"Why?" Matthew lifted a brow. "Because you're afraid she'll take us away? I heard Gammie say you don't have a leg to stand on if she decides to—"

"Now, that's about all I want to hear of what your gammie said or didn't say." Landon frowned. "Knowing Patricia, I feel sure you weren't supposed to hear any of that and as upset as she is, she probably didn't mean half of it anyway. You're not gonna keep throwing it out for the whole world to hear."

Matthew looked down. His fingers picked at a cut in the hardwood floor beneath his leg. "But you are afraid Aunt Katie'll take us away, aren't you? That's why you want me to be nice to her."

Nope. There was no way Katie would actually follow through on her guardianship responsibilities—especially after her small taste of parenthood today.

But…man. What was it about a kid's instincts that allowed them to see right through a cool facade and put their finger on the pulse of the one irrational fear you were trying to hide?

Landon blew out a heavy breath. Like it or not, he wasn't related to the kids in the legal sense. He was just a good friend of their parents. Katie had the legal right to call the shots when it came to the kids whether her decision was in their best interests or not, and that fact alone was enough to disconcert him.

"I want you to be nice to her because she's family," Landon said firmly. "No matter how many reasons you might have to think otherwise, she does care about you." And to be fair, she was trying to reconnect with the kids, which surprised even him. "She may not have always done the right things in the past, but who has? What matters is that she's trying to now."

Matthew slouched, a small grunt escaping him.

Well, Landon supposed silence was better than another angry outburst. He'd take it.

"That's enough talking for now. It's been a long couple of days and you need some rest." Landon eased to his feet then tugged Matthew to his. "Go jump in the shower, brush your teeth and get in the bed."

"Yes, sir."

"Hey." Landon opened his arms. "We don't go to bed angry around here."

Matthew huffed out a breath, hugged him briefly then trudged down the hallway into the bathroom.

Landon closed his eyes and kneaded the back of his neck, wondering when the hell this day would ever end. But there was one nagging thought that refused to be silenced.

Pulling his cell phone from his pocket, he left the house and walked out to the porch. The warm night air settled around him as he dialed a number.

Nate answered on the second ring. "Hey, man. I was just about to check in with you. Amber and I didn't have a chance to talk to you at the funeral yesterday. We've been worried. You and the kids doing okay?"

"As well as can be expected." Head aching, Landon rubbed his temples but managed a smile. As brothers-in-law went, Nate had turned out to be the best. Nate had always been more of a brother to him than a best friend—even before marrying his sister—but seeing him make Amber so happy had strengthened their friendship even more. "I've got a question for you."

"Shoot."

"How complicated does life become when you share a house with a woman?"

Dead silence fell over the connection. Landon's pulse quickened, the heavy throb echoing painfully in his skull, drowning out the chirps of crickets from the surrounding darkness.

Nate whistled low. "Well, now, what're we talking about here? A wife, girlfriend…?"

"Neither." Lord knows single-till-I-die Katie would scoff at both of those titles. "I'm talking about Katie."

Landon eyed a rut in the driveway, just visible by the weak porch light, where Katie's back car tire had spun on her way out last night. Considering her plans to stay in Elk Valley for one week or two, and her tendency for reckless driving, he'd bet there'd be thousands of ruts by the time she left if she accepted his offer to stay at the ranch with him and the kids.

An offer that he still wasn't exactly sure was a good idea.

"Katie," Nate repeated, a subtle note of confusion in his tone. "She sticking around? I thought she'd be on a plane back to California by now."

"You and me both." Landon sighed. "She decided to stay for a week or so and right now she's renting a room in town."

"And you're thinking of inviting her to your place?"

"'Fraid so. The kids and I met her for dinner tonight

and it didn't go so well. Matthew's not budging an inch for her and I'm hoping it'll help if I get her over here, give her some extra time with him."

"That's considerate," Nate said. "You take damn good care of those kids, too. Frank and Jennifer made the right decision leaving them with you."

"Yeah, well…" Landon bit his lip then said, "Turns out, I'm secondary guardian—Katie's the primary. That's the main reason I'm thinking of asking her over. I'm hoping it'll help her mend things with the kids and let her see how much better off they'll be with me in the long run."

"Well, hell. That does complicate things. Why didn't you tell me?"

"Katie didn't find out until she came home yesterday and I didn't want to tell anyone until she knew." Landon ignored the twinge of discomfort in his gut. "It's not that big a deal. Katie's not parent material and isn't interested in being one. Once she sees how well the kids will be taken care of here, she'll sign the papers and be on her way. It's just… I was prepared for the kids moving in, but not Katie, too. I've got my own routine and the kids have theirs. I'm just wondering if we can all make it through a week under the same roof together."

"Ah, a week's nothing." Nate sounded confident. "It'll fly by. But—" a small sound escaped him "—keep your bathroom, all right?"

Landon frowned. "What?"

"Your bathroom. It's a good idea to restrict her to the guest bathroom first thing, otherwise you'll end up with girlie stuff in every nook and cranny." Nate laughed. "I love your sister, but I can't brush my teeth in the morning without moving a comb, hair spray, body lotion and at least three tubes of lipstick. And that's just what's on the counter. Don't even get me started on the three inches of cabinet space I'm left with after she stuffed all her stuff in the vanity. Letting a woman in your bathroom will mess with your whole routine."

Landon cringed. "Guest bathroom, it is. Thanks."

"And Landon?"

"Yeah?"

Nate's voice was hesitant. "Not to risk your wrath again by bringing this up, but a couple years ago, I wasn't interested in or expecting to be a parent, either."

A wry smile crossed Landon's lips. He could laugh about it now, but two years ago when Amber, a single mom at the time, had kept the identity of her triplets' father a secret, he'd been shocked when she'd finally revealed that it was Nate. It was the first and only time he and Nate had ever come to blows—something Landon was still ashamed of.

As it turned out, Nate had been shocked by Amber's revelation, too. He hadn't known their one night together had resulted in triplets, but after Nate found out about the babies, he'd walked away from bull riding, ended his nomadic ways and proved to Amber how much he loved her and the kids. He'd eventually won her over and Landon had never seen Amber or Nate happier.

"I'm not trying to brag or anything," Nate continued, "but I think I've turned out to be a decent dad."

"And husband." Landon's smile returned full-force. "Brag all you want, man. I'll be the first to admit you're the best."

"But you wouldn't have two years ago," Nate said quietly.

No, Landon thought, he wouldn't have. Back then, he hadn't thought of fun-loving, free-living Nate as a good candidate for a husband or father, and neither had anyone else in Elk Valley. But Nate had proven them all wrong.

"All I'm saying is," Nate insisted, "don't judge Katie the same way people judged me."

Heading back inside the house, Landon chose not to respond to that and instead asked, "Do you mind driving over here and watching the kids for a bit? I'd like to drive into town and extend the invitation to Katie before I wimp out."

"Sure. It's the least I can do with you watching the triplets for us tomorrow. And speaking of that, you sure you're still up for babysitting? I mean, you've had a rough few days—"

"No, we're still on. You and Amber have had this planned for a month and need a day off. It'll do me and the kids good. Take our minds off things for a while."

"Yep." Nate chuckled. "My three troublemakers will take your mind off a lot of things."

"Hey, I can't think of anything else I'd rather do than spend time with my niece and nephews tomorrow."

Although thirty minutes later, Landon could think of several things he'd rather be doing than standing outside Katie's motel room at nine o'clock on a Saturday night, trying to summon the courage to follow through with his invitation.

Suck it up. This is the best thing for the kids. He lifted his fist to knock, but the door flew open, leaving him hitting air instead.

"What's happened? Is Matthew okay?"

Katie stood in the doorway, wrapped in a lavender bathrobe, cheeks pink, hair damp and skin smelling so damned delicious he had the sudden urge to bury his face against the smooth curve of her neck and inhale.

"I—" Catching himself leaning toward her, he jerked back and shoved his hands in his pockets. "Nothing's happened."

"You didn't call." She frowned. Those big brown eyes roved intensely over his face. "I've been pacing this room like a lunatic waiting to hear from you."

"I'm sorry."

He glanced at the nightly news blaring on the TV, the purple cell phone charging on the dresser, the hairline crack in the ceiling—anything to keep his attention off the soft swell of her cleavage above the robe's V and the toned length of her legs below the short hem.

"Matthew's fine," he said.

An open laptop rested on the double bed beside rumpled sheets. Several candy wrappers, what looked like the melted remains of a banana split in a plastic bowl and an empty soda bottle littered the foot of the bed. Clothing was strewn across the floor. There were jeans, inside out, by the nightstand. A wadded-up T-shirt, socks and sneakers next to the dresser. And a lace bra and pink underwear tangled together on the threshold of the bathroom.

Oh, man. What a mess.

He smoothed a shaky hand over his collar and looked beyond the discarded lingerie to the bathroom's interior. There was a steamed-up mirror, a dozen colorful spheres the size of tennis balls filled the empty sink and covered the counter and that tantalizing scent he'd noticed on Katie's skin wafted from the tub where her shapely, tanned body had probably reclined just prior to his arrival.

What a mess. Landon swallowed hard. What a sinfully, sexy m—

"The kids are fine," he blurted out. "I just came by to invite you to spend the night with me."

She blinked, her brow furrowing.

"I mean, us. The kids. Stay at the ranch." He shifted from one foot to the other. *Make complete sentences, numbskull.* "There's no sense in you renting a motel room for a week when you can stay at the ranch for free. It'd give you more time with the kids and might improve things between you and Matthew. I think having you there will help alleviate their shock at losing Frank and Jennifer the way they did. You're not obligated to accept, but the offer's there all the same."

Landon nodded. There. Fully formed, logical sentences born of sound common sense and delivered with grace, placing the ball firmly in her court.

Katie moved to speak then hesitated. "But my mom. Those things she said…"

"That was grief talking. Knowing Patricia, I feel sure those were words she never meant for the kids— or you—to hear." Landon rolled his shoulders. "Patricia has a bad habit of being overly critical of everyone— myself included. Something you're already familiar with, yeah?"

She looked down, her features relaxing, but sadness entered her eyes as she nodded.

"No matter what anyone says or doesn't say," he continued, "those kids need you."

Katie looked up. "You think so?"

Her hopeful expression and hesitant smile tugged at something deep inside him. A latent longing warred with the twinge of guilt pricking his skin. *Easy...* This was only temporary, and the kids were better off staying here with him. It was important she understood that.

He took a small step forward, carefully weighing his words. "Right now, they do. You're family. They need all the family they can get."

That tiny smile faded. "Right," she whispered.

Her gaze lowered again and she curled her bare toes into the thin carpet.

"Hey." He nudged her chin up with a knuckle. "There's only one Katydid, and we'd love to have you with us. I feel sure Matthew will come around before the week is up."

That hopeful gleam returned and tears brimmed on her long lashes. She flashed a gorgeous smile then threw her arms around him, plastering every fragrant inch of her tempting body against his.

"Thank you, thank you, thank you." She pulled back, bouncing. "You have no idea how much that would mean to me."

Then she laid one on him.

Dear sweet heaven. The strong press of her warm mouth against his lips, her light breath against his cheek and her low hum of appreciation rocked Landon to his core—and back on his heels. He stumbled slightly, one hand shooting out to grab the door frame and the other gripping her elbow to steady them both.

She sprang back. Her fingers clutched the lapels of her robe high against her neck and her eyes widened. "S-sorry. I shouldn't have done that." Her lush lips trembled. "Well, I should've thanked you—and I did—but I shouldn't have…you know. It was an impulse," she finished quickly.

Yep. Impulses and Katie were inseparable. He rolled his lips together. Her sweet taste touched his tongue, stoking heat low in his belly, and his palms tingled, wanting to part the robe, slide over her bare skin and cup her curves.

"My bathroom's off-limits." His voice was tight. He cleared his throat and tried again. "I mean, you can have the guest room and share the hall bathroom with the kids. But my bedroom, bathroom and personal space are all private. And I like to keep my place neat, you know?"

She held up her hands, palms out, and nodded. "Of course."

He spun on his heels. "I'll wait for you in the truck."

"I'll be packed and ready in five minutes." The cheerful pep returned to Katie's voice. "Thank you for this. I'll be the perfect houseguest and I'll pitch in and earn my keep. I promise you won't regret it."

Landon strode across the parking lot on desire-weakened legs, his nerves cringing with the distinct realization that he already did.

Chapter 4

Katie shoved a pitchfork beneath a pile of manure, shook off the shavings then dumped the waste into a wheelbarrow. "Seven stalls down, three more to go."

Straightening, she dragged the back of her arm across her sweaty brow and glanced at the row of stalls to her left. With a little luck and a lot of prayer, she just might manage to fulfill her promise to Landon by earning her keep for her first night's stay at his ranch. Then she'd still be able to spend the rest of the day with Matthew, who hadn't looked at all happy when Landon had brought her to the ranch last night, and, hopefully, make a little headway with him.

But, good Lord, when had she gotten so out of shape? And weak? And...*ew*. Her arm stilled against her forehead. When had her deodorant worn off?

"Making progress?"

Katie jerked her arm down to her side and spun around.

Landon stood in the entrance to the stable, the strong late-morning sun highlighting his muscular frame and Rascal panting at his heels. "You've been out here since eight this morning. It's almost eleven thirty. You all right?"

"Yep." Lower back aching, she rubbed it and forced a smile. "Just earning my keep like I promised I would."

Though to be honest, had she known how odorous and muscle-twinging mucking stalls would be, she'd have suggested an easier, more pleasant-smelling chore. Especially on a Sunday.

She puffed a strand of sweaty hair out of her face. "Can I ask you something?"

"Sure."

"Does it normally take this long to muck the stalls?"

"No." His lips twitched. "Not normally."

Her shoulders drooped. "Of course." Only her inept attempts would stretch a quick task into a long one. "I swear I'll be done within the hour."

Landon shook his head. "I told you this wasn't necessary. You're our guest, not a ranch hand."

"But I promised I wasn't going to mooch off you and I meant it."

"So to you, that means mucking ten stalls on your own after five hours of sleep?" He lifted an eyebrow. "It was three o'clock in the morning before I stopped hearing the water running in the guest bathroom."

She made a face. "Sorry. I was trying to squeeze in a little extra work before bed."

And take her mind off how much she missed Jennifer. But she'd failed miserably at both.

It'd been impossible to test the performance and fragrances of Sandra's new line of bath bombs in Landon's guest bathroom. Each time she'd sudsed up the tiny sink, she'd had to rinse it down and air out the room for ten minutes before trying the next one, otherwise the scents were too difficult to discern and evaluate, much less name.

What she really needed was a roomy tub like the one at the motel. At least there she could take a bath and test drive the bubbles instead. Here, the only way to fit her six-foot frame in the guest room bathtub would be to sit with her knees bent to her eyebrows and stay that way.

Forget that!

Landon eyed her. "Exactly what brand are you managing that keeps you up to that time of night?"

Hmm. There was that tone again. The slightly disapproving one with a tinge of sarcasm that she could do without. "Sandra's Sexy Suds."

His blond eyebrow arched higher.

"Now, don't get all uptight again." Sighing, she leaned on the pitchfork at her side. "They're bath bubbles in colorful, solid spheres, not alcohol or see-through panties. Make sure you tell my mother that when she asks—which I'm sure she will. If you don't, she'll go around telling everyone in Elk Valley that I've brought shame to the family by brewing demonic beer that strips you of your inhibitions and sewing sex-inducing underwear that encourages hedonism."

Katie stomped the heel of her sneaker against the ground, knocking off a clump of dirt and wishing for the millionth time that Jennifer was still with her. Jennifer always understood and supported her no matter what dream she chased, and Jennifer would've defended her against any judgmental criticism from their mom. She also would've been the first to volunteer to take the bubble baths for a test drive and they would've had a blast.

Oh, that was it. She missed Jennifer's laughter the most. The way her optimism had shone in her smile and forgiving nature. How she always managed to see past the bad in others and admire the good everyone else missed. Even her own.

At Landon's continued silence, Katie asked, "Don't tell me—you disapprove of my career choice, too? And you think my staying up until three in the morning is just one more reason why I would make an unsuitable parent."

"I didn't say that."

"You didn't have to." She lifted her chin. "I work hard and won't apologize for that. It took me a long time to find a job I loved—to discover work I was passionate about. And I feel good when I help someone achieve their own dream. I don't owe anyone a justification for the career I've chosen."

Landon walked over, studied her face then drew the pad of his forefinger over the soft skin beneath her eyes. "But you look like you could use a good night's sleep. That's all I'm saying. I didn't mean to suggest anything other than that."

"Oh." She sagged against the pitchfork. "Sor—"

"No need to apologize. I'm just asking you to consider slowing down a bit. At least while you're here. Take a break for once and focus on getting over your loss. Focus on the kids."

And there it was.

She bristled. "That's exactly why I'm here."

His strong jaw clenched, his gaze falling to her lips, his thick lashes lowering over his eyes. And she wondered what he was thinking. If he felt that strong pull in his belly like she had in that moment last night at the motel when she'd recognized the same pain in his eyes and wanted to touch him, seek comfort...heal.

Or if he remembered her haphazard kiss and if his mouth still felt bare and vulnerable like hers. If maybe—just maybe— he'd invited her here because her presence was comforting in light of their shared grief?

Probably not. Landon had never been the kind of guy to be swayed by emotion. He believed in good deeds and moral actions. Her plight fit both of those categories.

Katie withdrew from his touch. "My focus *is* on Matthew, Emma and Sophia. No matter what my job obligations are, that won't change."

He stepped back and shoved his hands in his pockets. "Matthew and I finished feeding and turning the horses out. We're taking Emma and Sophia for a walk until Amber and Nate drop the kids off, then I'll start lunch. Why don't you take a break and join us?"

Wheels crunched over gravel and a giggle rang out. She craned her neck and peered over Landon's shoulder.

Matthew and Emma stood outside the stable's entrance, each of them rocking Sophia forward and backward in a stroller. Sophia, clad in a blue polka-dot dress, grinned and kicked her bare feet with every push. Lots of sunshine, green fields and warm, fresh air lay just beyond.

Emma blew a bubble with her chewing gum then smiled and called out, "Come walk with us, Aunt Katie."

"Who could resist that sweet face?" Katie laughed and propped the pitchfork against a stall door. "And it'll sure beat shoveling poop, so yes, and thank you for the invitation. But—" she held up her pointer finger and narrowed her eyes at Landon "—I'm going to come back and finish the last three stalls after lunch."

One corner of his mouth lifted in a sexy tilt. "If you insist."

They walked the perimeter of Landon's house, strolling across lush grass past the wooden deck attached to the back. Katie stopped to pet Rascal and admired the view from the steps.

Hay fields stretched unimpeded toward a misty mountain range that met the sky. Golden sunlight spilled over the valley and she had the strangest urge to dash across the green paddocks until her lungs burned and laugh out loud like a kid.

"This is beautiful," Katie said.

Landon continued walking, holding hands with Emma. "It pales in comparison to your parents' place. You could walk for days there and still be on the property."

"Yes, but their place doesn't have the same feel to it." She swept an arm toward the rocking chairs on the deck. "And they don't have a front-row view like this."

"Uncle Landon made the deck by himself," Emma said, bouncing at his side.

Landon ruffled Matthew's hair. "You helped build it, too, didn't you, buddy?"

Matthew shrugged.

"That's awesome." Katie quickened her step to reach Matthew's side then smiled at him. "I didn't know you were into construction."

He stared down at Sophia's stroller then mumbled, "You don't know much of anything about me."

Katie glanced at Landon who shook his head. "But I'd like to," she said. "What else have you buil—"

A horn honked in rapid succession, blaring out a playful tune.

Matthew nudged Sophia's stroller toward Landon then ran off, calling over his shoulder, "Aunt Amber's here."

Well. So much for a bit of bonding. Katie sighed then followed Landon and Emma to the front lawn.

It'd been three years since Katie had last seen Amber and Nate. Amber hadn't aged a bit. She still had long, blond hair, blue eyes and a killer smile. Though with Nate by her side, she glowed from the inside with happiness, and every adoring glance the muscular man at her side cast down at her made her smile wider.

Nate, blond, tall and built, was every bit as handsome as Katie remembered.

"It's so good to see you, Katie." Amber hugged her then whispered in her ear, "I just wish it were under better circumstances. Jennifer was a wonderful woman. If there's anything I can do…"

Katie returned the hug then stepped back, blinking away a fresh sheen of tears. "Thank you. Being here helps. It was good of Landon to invite me."

"That's Landon, all right," Nate said, lifting a third toddler from the back seat of a SUV and setting him on his feet beside another boy and girl the same age. "Considerate. Staid and dependable."

Landon looked away, an odd look of displeasure crossing his face. "Don't wear yourself out on the compliments, Nate."

Nate flashed a mischievous grin. "What?"

"You make me sound like someone's stuffy grandpa."

"Okay. How 'bout strong, courteous and fantastic dad material?" Nate winked at Katie then glanced down at the blond triplets standing at his feet. "Whatcha think, kids? A woman would be lucky to get ahold of your uncle Landon, wouldn't they?"

Oh, great. Katie tucked her hair behind her ear and avoided Landon's eyes. Just what they needed. Another well-meaning family member meddling in their already uncomfortable situation.

Landon's disgruntled groan made her cheeks burn hotter.

"Cut it out, Nate." Amber nudged him with her elbow then muttered, "You're embarrassing them." She smiled at Katie. "Let me introduce you to our gang of two-year-olds."

The two boys stared up at her, eyes curious. The little girl between them grinned.

"This is our adventurous Mason." Amber tapped one blond head then another. "This is our strong, silent Dylan. And this—" she urged the little girl forward "—is our little diva, Savannah. Go say hello, sweetie."

Katie grinned as Savannah toddled over, her blond curls rippling in the breeze, cheeks rosy and pink overalls the cutest things she'd ever seen. She crouched and beckoned Savannah closer, imagining how much fun it might be to play with kids who had no preconceived notions about her.

"Hi, Savannah. It's nice to meet you."

Savannah steadied herself with a hand on Katie's knee. She picked a straw of hay from Katie's jeans then looked up, her nose wrinkling. "Stink."

Amber gasped. *"Savannah."*

Oh, Lord. How embarrassing—but brutally true.

Katie smiled and waved Amber's concern away. "It's okay, Savannah's just being honest. I spent the morning working in the stable." She returned her attention to Savannah and shrugged helplessly. "I apologize. I assure you I smelled much better four hours ago and, normally, I smell just fine. It's just today, you know?"

Savannah lost interest. She flung the hay on the ground then ran to Landon, chortling, her arms outstretched. "Up, Unc Andon."

He complied, propped her on his hip and kissed her cheek. "There's my gorgeous girl."

Laughter tinged his voice and the kind adoration in his tone made Katie appreciate the sight of him even more. No doubt Nate was right. Landon would make a great father...and husband.

Oh, no. None of that. Katie shoved to her feet. Landon was hot—she'd admit it—but he wasn't why she was here. And he didn't own the title of Good Parent to the exclusion of everyone else. She could be just as good with kids if she put her mind to it.

"Thanks again for watching them," Amber said, smiling at Landon. "We'll be back in a couple of hours."

Landon frowned. "I thought y'all had planned to drive up the mountain for the day."

"We did," Nate added. "But all things considered, a couple hours is enough of a break for us. We decided to drive into town, have a relaxed lunch then swing back by and pick them up."

Landon shook his head. "You don't have to cut your trip short. I'm happy to watch them."

Nate held up one hand as he opened the SUV's passenger door for Amber with another. "Trust me, two hours of uninterrupted conversation and a finished meal without three toddlers *is* a break for me and Amber. Plus—" he cast a sympathetic look at Katie "—I figured y'all could use some peace and quiet this afternoon."

Katie glanced at Landon, the sadness she felt welling back up inside her reflected in his expression. He nodded, waved them off then smiled at the five kids on the ground and the one in his arms. "Let's go inside and grab a bite to eat."

"Then we can play?" Emma asked, chasing Mason, who laughed as he chased Rascal around Sophia's stroller.

"Yep." Landon gestured in Matthew's direction. "Bring Sophia in and help your aunt Katie put her in the high chair, okay?"

Scowling, Matthew dropped his head but pushed Sophia's stroller toward the house. "Whatever."

Twenty minutes later, they had just sat down at the kitchen table to eat sandwiches Landon had prepared when his cell phone rang. He left the room briefly then returned, frowning as he shoved his phone into his back pocket.

"That was Nate's brother, Mac."

For a second, Katie's heart froze. "Are Amber and Nate okay?"

Landon smiled as he sat at the table. "They're fine. Mac was calling about his ranch. One of the horses kicked out a fence and six of them escaped. With Nate gone, he needs an extra hand rounding them up. Nate suggested he call me. Said Nate thought I could leave the kids with you for an hour and help him out."

A wave of terror rippled through Katie. She glanced around the table. The triplets sat quietly in their booster seats, eating the ham and sliced grapes Landon had set in front of them. Emma hummed as she spooned pureed carrots into Sophia's grinning mouth and Matthew narrowed his eyes at her as he chewed a bite of his sandwich.

The kids were relaxed and content. And Landon would only be gone for what? An hour, he'd said? What could go wrong?

"Yeah," Katie said slowly. "That'd be fine."

Landon's hands stilled halfway to his mouth, a tomato sliding from his sandwich and plopping onto his plate. "What'd you say?"

"I said that'd be fine. Go ahead."

He stared. "You're kidding, right?" He leaned closer and lowered his voice. "You want me to leave you alone with six kids?"

She straightened in her seat. "It's only for an hour. It'll take us at least half that to finish lunch, so it won't be for long anyway."

A laugh burst from his lips. "No way." He turned back to his sandwich. "Forget it."

Oh, boy. That had hurt. Much more than she'd expected it to.

"Why? Because you don't trust me? Because you think I'm irresponsible?"

Catching herself, Katie stilled and glanced at the kids. Emma and Matthew were enthralled, looking from her to Landon then back.

Leaning closer, she whispered in his ear, "I'm not a loser, Landon. I'm perfectly capable of watching six kids for one hour."

"I didn't mean to—" He winced, sneaked a glance at the kids then mumbled, "All right."

Reluctance laced his tone, but Katie smiled anyway. It was, at the very least, a step in the right direction. "Great."

"You still have my cell phone number, right?" At her nod, he slowly stood. "Call me if you need something. And I mean *anything*. And if something serious happens, call 91—"

"Yes, yes, yes. Now get out." Katie shoved him toward the door and exchanged a laugh with Emma. "We'll be perfectly fine."

Landon kissed the kids then walked away, hesitating on the threshold of the kitchen to look back at the kids before exiting the house.

After he left, Katie grabbed a napkin and held it out toward Emma. "Gum, please, Emma. You can't chew a sandwich with gum in your mouth."

Emma smiled, a look of pride in her eyes, and plucked her gum out.

Katie reached for it, but Savannah's sippy cup slipped from her hand and clattered to the floor, prompting Savannah to cry and struggle to reach it. Sighing, Katie squatted between the chairs and retrieved the cup, rinsed it in the sink then returned it to Savannah.

She held the napkin back out to Emma. "Okay. I'll take your gum now."

Emma frowned. "I already gave it to you."

Katie looked at the empty napkin. "No, you didn't."

"Yes, I did." She opened her mouth to prove her point then picked up her sandwich.

"Then where did it go?" Katie asked, searching the floor.

Emma shrugged and continued eating. Matthew smirked.

The sippy cup hit the floor again and Savannah resumed crying. Startled, Sophia joined her. Mason and Dylan covered their ears, climbed down from their booster seats then toddled off down the hall.

Welp. Katie twisted her hands. This hour might be more challenging than she'd thought.

Three hours after Landon left home, he returned.

He got out of his truck, eyed the silent surroundings then blew out a breath as he stared at his house. "Still standing."

Thank the good Lord. After helping Mac round up half of the missing horses, he'd called Katie's cell phone to check in, knowing the task at hand would take longer than the estimated hour. She'd answered on the second ring, her voice strained, but had insisted everything was fine.

He'd asked to speak to Matthew who'd answered his concerned questions with one-word responses and a subtle hint of amusement. Speaking to Emma hadn't helped much, either. Laughter and a breathless *"Gotta go"* had been all he'd received before the connection had been severed.

It'd taken every ounce of polite upbringing and self-restraint he possessed not to leap in his truck, gun the engine and fly back to the ranch to see for himself that the kids were okay. But that would fracture the tenuous trust he'd tried to establish with Katie. Not to mention it would undermine the very reason for bringing her to the ranch in the first place. He'd wanted her to spend time with the kids and, like it or not, that's exactly what he'd left her to do for three hours.

Picking up his pace, he walked across the front lawn, ascended the steps then stopped abruptly on the porch.

Rascal sat by a rocking chair, licking his paw. An orange substance speckled his brown fur and a thick glob of it rested on top of his head.

"Whatcha got there, buddy?" Landon bent close and sniffed. It smelled familiar. Kinda like… "Did you get into Sophia's carrots?"

Rascal lifted his head, licked Landon's cheek then resumed cleaning his paw.

Groaning, Landon scrubbed his cheek with the sleeve of his T-shirt. Yeah. Definitely carrots.

He followed the crooked trail of orange goo from the porch through the front entrance and into the living room. The TV blared the upbeat pings and booms of a video game. Matthew and Emma were stretched out on the floor, eyes on the screen and their fingers flying over game controllers.

"Where's Katie?" Landon asked.

Neither one of them stopped playing or looked at him but Emma lifted her chin and said, "Sophia's room."

"The triplets?"

Matthew answered this time. "Aunt Amber and Uncle Nate picked them up an hour ago."

"Why is Rascal covered in Sophia's lunch?"

Emma giggled. "He jumped on the kitchen table when Aunt Katie chased Mason and Dylan outside."

Landon froze. "Why was she chasing Mason and Dylan?"

"Because they got the front door open and ran away while she was changing Sophia's diaper." Emma glanced over her shoulder and smiled. "They wanted to play."

Aw, man. He'd forgotten about the diapers. Had Katie ever changed one before?

"I'm going to check on Sophia. You two—" he pointed at them "—don't move."

No chance of that. They'd already been sucked back into their video game trance.

Heart pounding, Landon eased down the hallway and into Sophia's room. Baby wipes, a dozen mangled diapers and four onesies littered the bedroom floor. A thick layer of baby powder coated the changing table, a portion of the carpet and the nightstand.

"Good night above."

Shaking his head, Landon crossed the room and peeked inside the crib where Sophia slept peacefully— and in one piece—then glanced at the nearby rocking chair. Katie was sprawled in it, sound asleep, her head resting at a crooked angle and one arm slung over the crib's top railing.

Baby powder and pureed carrots stained the front of her T-shirt. Her dark hair was mussed, her pink lips were parted and her chest lifted on deep, even breaths. She looked exhausted and it'd be a shame to wake her. Still, he wouldn't be doing her any favors by letting her get a crick in her neck.

He lowered to his haunches and drifted his thumb across her flushed cheek. "Katie, wake up."

Her thick lashes lifted, fluttering softly against his fingertip as she opened her eyes and focused on his face. "Oh, no. I didn't mean to fall asleep." She blinked hard then struggled to sit upright. Panic flickered across her expression. "Are the kids all right?"

"They're fine." He lowered his hand, squeezing her knee to calm her. "Sophia's sleeping and Matthew and Emma are playing video games."

"What time is it?"

"Three thirty."

"In the morning?"

He grinned. "In the afternoon. Matthew said Nate and Amber picked up the triplets an hour ago, so I'm guessing you fell asleep after that?"

Katie nodded, a dazed look in her eyes. "They asked about you. I told them it took longer than you thought to round up the horses." She looked down and red blotches spread across her neck. "I think your sister thinks I'm incompetent. I mean, she was nice and all, but she just gave me this look as though…"

"As though what?"

"Everything went okay for a while, and then things just kind of fell apart." Her voice trembled. "I don't know what happened. The kids were all okay but it was…" She spread her hands, searching for the right word.

"Overwhelming?" he asked.

She nodded slowly. "Landon?"

"Hmm?"

"You were right."

"About what?"

"I am a loser." Her cute face crumpled. "And I have gum in my hair."

He rolled his lips together and stifled a laugh. Her eyes were puffy and red, and tears spilled down her face, but even so, she was damned adorable. "Where?"

Her breath caught on a sob. "What?"

"Where in your hair is the gum?"

"Above my right ear." Her hand lifted then stilled in midair, a horrified expression crossing her face. "I'll have to shave my head."

She doubled over, her shoulders jerking on heavier sobs.

"No, you won't." Smiling, he rubbed her back in slow circles. "We'll get it out."

"H-how?"

"A little trick I learned. Come on." He scooped one arm under her knees and the other around her back then stood and lifted her to his chest. "It'll be out in five minutes, tops."

She buried her damp face against his neck and looped her arms tight around his shoulders as he carried her farther down the hallway and into his bathroom. He tried his best to ignore how good she felt in his arms.

"Sit here for a minute," he said, lowering her to the edge of his tub. "I'll be right back."

He waited until she balanced herself into a seated position then went to the kitchen and grabbed a jar of peanut butter. When he returned, he sat beside her and sifted through her hair until he found the gum.

She wiped her face with the back of her hand. "Peanut butter?"

"Yep." He scooped a small portion out of the jar and applied it to her hair, rubbing the strands between his fingertips. "Had to do the same thing for Emma last year."

After saturating the sticky knot in her hair, he set the jar aside and washed his hands in the sink.

"You said I wasn't allowed in your bathroom," she whispered.

He caught her eyes on him in the mirror and smiled. "Today, I'll make an exception. Might even consider letting you use the tub."

She smiled back. "Because I stink like horse poo, carrots and peanut butter?"

Laughing, he grabbed a comb and sat beside her. "Nah."

Quite the opposite, in fact.

He placed a hand on her soft hair and combed in gentle sweeps. The scent of hay, horse hide and sun-warmed honeysuckle—a mix he remembered best from his childhood summers in Elk Valley—released with each movement. She relaxed and eased back against his chest, the soft weight of her sending a pleasurable tingle through him.

"You smell like home," he said softly.

She twisted against him, looking over her shoulder. "Like what?"

He cleared his throat and continued combing. "The hay in your hair. It reminds me of playing in the stable when I was kid. Like the outdoors in springtime. It's familiar and earthy. Nostalgic, I guess."

"Oh." Her eyes grew heavy as she gazed at him. Her upper body swayed with the slow rhythm of his hand in her hair. "I don't think I can do this."

He stared at her mouth, wanting to part her lips with his. To taste her again. "Do what?"

"Be a good aunt or a good mom." Her chin trembled. "Matthew's right. I don't know the first thing about him, Emma or Sophia. I don't have a clue how to reach them."

This was his chance. The moment he'd been hoping for when he'd invited her to stay with them, and it had come much sooner than he'd expected. All he had to do was agree, reassure her the kids were better off with him, then she'd leave next week.

But that would also leave the kids with one less dependable adult in their lives. Another loss of someone who loved them.

Landon wished he could remain silent, watch Katie fail at being a good parent and not feel guilty. Only, it wasn't about what he wanted—it was about Matthew, Emma and Sophia.

"Instead of using your head," he whispered, "use your heart."

Chapter 5

Use your heart.

Katie combed her hair once then smoothed a hand over it and smiled. "Back to normal."

Better than normal—fantastic. For once, she actually liked her glossy, stick-straight hair better than the artificial curls it took an hour to perfect.

She turned right in front of Landon's bathroom mirror then left, studying the way the lights danced over the dark strands and trying to decide what had changed her mind.

Maybe it was hard work on a ranch that made the difference. After her mini-breakdown last night, a long soak in Landon's tub and a good night's rest, she'd hopped out of bed at five this morning, mucked all ten stalls in the stables in under two hours—*thank you very much!*—and bathed and dressed again in time for breakfast with the kids at seven fifteen.

Those seemingly small accomplishments had done a ton to improve her self-confidence and plant her feet back on the ground. But it could've been something else...

She closed her eyes, her palm drifting back to her hair, her fingers weaving through the soft ends. Maybe it was that the gentle pressure of Landon's big hand still tingled on her scalp. That the firm strength of his arms lifting and enfolding her still made her body hum with pleasure. Or it might've been the low throb of his voice when he'd leaned close and whispered, *You smell like home...familiar, earthy.*

Her eyes sprang open. "That's it!"

She tossed the comb on the counter then plundered through her overnight bag for a pen and scrap piece of paper. Finding one, she scrawled *Be at Home*, dug around some more until she found a beige bath bomb then sat both on a medicine shelf above the sink, the paper propped against the bath sphere.

"A subtle earthy scent housed in a neutral beige that conjures up nostalgic thoughts of home paired with a title that reflects exactly that." She whistled low. "Perfect."

Now she just had to come up with names for the other colorful bath bombs filling her overnight bag. Nodding, she grabbed her bag, dropped it off in the guest room then made her way to the kitchen.

Landon and the kids sat around the table, eating breakfast. The aroma of bacon and syrup made her stomach growl.

"Something smells delicious." Katie sat beside Emma and kissed her cheek.

Emma grinned around a mouthful. "Uncle Landon made us pancakes."

"That was nice of him." Katie smiled as Landon nudged a plate of pancakes and bacon in her direction. "Thank you for this and for letting me use your tub again this morning."

His attention roved over her hair, face and mouth before he met her eyes. "You're welcome. You look very nice."

The male appreciation in his tone shot a thrill through her. "Thanks. I hope you don't mind that I hand-washed a few items of clothing in there, too. I hung them in your bathroom to dry but I'll be sure to get them out this afternoon."

A wary look entered his eyes. He moved to speak but seemed to think better of it and returned to feeding Sophia pureed peaches. "That's fine."

Katie turned to Matthew who pushed bits of pancake around his plate with a fork. "Good morning, Matthew."

He looked up briefly, his brown eyes disapproving, then stared down at his plate. "Morning."

Katie bit into a crisp strip of bacon and consoled herself with the fact that he'd at least acknowledged her presence.

"Are you going to school with us?" Emma asked.

Katie sipped her coffee. "What do you mean?"

"Uncle Landon's driving us to school today instead of us riding the bus." Emma licked syrup from her lips and swung her legs against her chair.

"It's their first day back," Landon said quietly, meeting Katie's eyes across the table.

Their first day...since losing Jennifer and Frank.

Katie's bright mood dimmed. "Oh." She glanced at Matthew. His expression darkened and he stabbed the pancake harder. "I see. I'd love to go, if it's okay with you, Landon?"

"Sure." Landon wiped Sophia's chin then stood. "Soon as y'all finish, we'll get going. We need to have them there by eight."

Thirty minutes later, they arrived at Elk Valley Elementary. The halls smelled the same as Katie remembered—sharpened pencils, crayons and pungent cleaner—but everything seemed so much smaller. Katie towered over kids as they walked across the lobby to the front office. And boy, oh, boy, kids were everywhere: streaming from buses by the sidewalk, filing past the windows of the office in crooked lines, and one stood behind the reception desk, scowling as the secretary wiped his face.

"You've been told a thousand times not to throw food in the cafeteria during breakfast, Heath," the secretary said, scrubbing a stubborn stain off his cheek. "Go sit over there and wait until Mr. Waterson calls you."

The little boy—Heath, Katie supposed—trudged over to a line of chairs, plopped onto one then, when the secretary turned away, stuck out his tongue.

Katie laughed.

The glass partition slid back and the secretary stared at her through narrowed eyes. "May I help you?"

Katie stopped laughing. "Yes, please. I'm here with—"

"Me." Landon joined her, adjusting Sophia to a more

comfortable position on his hip, Matthew and Emma by his side. "We're dropping Matthew and Emma off."

The secretary's expression brightened. "Landon. It's so good to see you again."

"How are you, Melody?"

"Oh, just fine." She smiled and smoothed a hand over her blond hair. "Wonderful now, in fact."

Of course. Another Landon admirer.

Katie managed not to roll her eyes as the other woman simpered. Instead, she wrote off the jealous churn in her stomach as a side effect of eating too many pancakes, leaned to the side and waved at the little boy staring back at her from his seat outside the principal's office.

He waved back.

"We've been thinking about all of you," Melody whispered, leaning closer to Landon. "I'm so glad Matthew and Emma are back with us."

"About that." Landon leaned in, too. "We'd like you to keep an eye out for them for the first week or so. Maybe give us a call if you notice either one of them feeling down or not their usual self?"

"Us?" Melody asked, brow furrowing.

"Us." He motioned toward Katie. "Me and their aunt. You remember Katie Richards, Jennifer's younger sister?"

"Of course." Melody smiled in apology. "It's been so long, I didn't recognize you. I'm sorry for your loss."

Katie nodded. "Thank you."

"I'll be happy to keep an eye out," Melody said, facing Matthew and Emma. "We're so glad to have y'all back. Would it be okay if I walked with you two to class?"

Emma smiled. "Yes, ma'am."

Matthew rolled his eyes and flounced toward the door.

"Matthew," Landon called. When Matthew glanced over his shoulder, he added, "Try to have a good day, okay? If you need us, call us."

He kept walking and didn't answer.

Katie studied Landon's expression as he watched Matthew leave, the sadness clouding his eyes making her chest ache. "He'll be okay." She touched his upper arm. "And if he's not, we'll be here for him."

We. She turned the word over in her mind. It had a nice ring to it.

Landon looked at her, a small smile appearing. "Right."

Forty-five minutes later, Katie stood in the nursery, listening as Landon gave her tips on changing Sophia's diaper, when his cell phone rang.

He stilled, one hand clutching a baby wipe and the other cradling Sophia's heels in the air. "You mind getting that?"

"Sure." Katie glanced at the nightstand. "Where is it?"

He jerked his chin toward his butt. "Back pocket."

"O...kay."

She slipped her hand inside a pocket, searching delicately for the ringing phone and trying not to notice how firm and tempting his buttocks felt pressed against the denim. It was a downright sin for a man to have a butt this fine.

He glanced over his shoulder at her, one eyebrow arched and the corner of his mouth lifting in a small smile.

"G-got it." Face burning, she jerked the phone out of his pocket and accepted the call. "Hello?"

"May I speak with Landon Eason, please?"

Katie watched Landon slide a clean diaper under Sophia. "He's busy at the moment. Can I take a message?"

"This is Melody from Elk Valley Elementary. Is this Katie?"

"Yes. What's wrong? Has something happened to the kids?"

"Nothing major," Melody said, "but Matthew's had a small incident and the principal asked if you or Landon could meet with him at the school?"

Katie headed for the door. "I'm on my way."

"Wait, who was that?"

She paused on the threshold then held the phone out to Landon. "The school. Something's happened with Matthew. They want one of us to come."

"Here. Take Sophia and I'll—"

"No." Katie winced. "Please, Landon. Let me go?"

He looked hesitant, but after glancing back at Sophia, who grinned and reached out for him, he nodded. "All right. Just call me and let me know what's going on."

"Will do."

She made record time on the road and, after arriving at the elementary school fifteen minutes later, jogged from the parking lot into the front office. "I'm back."

"So soon." Melody smiled and opened the door to the inner office. "Matthew's fine. He's in Mr. Waterson's office now. If you'll please have a seat, I'll let them know you're here."

Katie thanked her then sat in one of the chairs lined

against the wall. She bit her nail and bounced her knee, straining to hear Melody's conversation in a nearby room.

"Are you scared?"

Katie glanced to her left. Heath, apparently, still waited for his turn with the principal. She managed a smile. "No. Just worried, I guess. You?"

He cringed. "A little. What'd you do?"

Her smile widened as she mulled over her school days. "Too much to name."

Heath turned away, eyes widening as he whistled. "Then you're really gonna get it."

Melody returned. "Come on in, Katie."

She did, anxiously searching Matthew's downcast expression as she sat beside him across from the principal.

"Thank you for coming, Ms. Richards." The principal, young and handsome with a friendly face, held out his hand. "I'm Clint Waterson."

Katie shook his hand. "Please call me Katie. What's happened?"

"On the way to class this morning, Matthew tore several posters off the wall and ripped them up." Clint eased back in his leather chair. "Students spent several weeks making them and it'll take days to create replacements."

"Matthew?"

He wouldn't look at her or the principal.

"Matthew knows he did wrong and apologized," Clint continued. "But I thought it was important you knew what he'd done and why."

Katie spread her hands and searched Matthew's expression. "Why *did* you do it?"

Matthew picked at a loose thread on his jeans. "They were posters for the spring festival."

She frowned. "And?" He grew silent again. "Matthew, I can't help if y—"

"We were supposed to sing." Matthew's head shot up and tears poured over his red cheeks. "Mom was leading the school chorus. She was gonna play the piano and we were supposed to sing together." His breath caught. "She promised."

Katie's throat closed. "Oh, Matthew. I'm sorry." Hand shaking, she squeezed his shoulder. "If your mom would've had a choice, she would've been here. I know she would have."

Matthew shook off her touch and turned away, his chest jerking on silent sobs.

Katie sagged back in her chair. She glanced at Clint, who grimaced and look down at his desk.

Oh, no. What in the world should she say now? What should she do? Or, better yet, what would Jennifer do? Or Landon? Katie reached into her pocket, curled her fingers around her cell phone then stilled. Landon's soft words from last night returned, drifting through her mind.

Instead of using your head, use your heart.

"I'll do it."

Katie froze. The words had left her lips and filled the silent room before she'd had a chance to stop them.

"Excuse me?" Clint asked.

Oh, boy. Why did she say that? She could kick herself for having such a big mouth.

But if she took it back now…

Katie looked at Matthew, pulled in a deep breath and sat up straighter. "I said I'll do it. I volunteer to lead the school chorus in place of my sister. I'll play the piano. And I'll sing with Matthew."

Clint's brows rose. "Have you ever done something like this before?"

"Music, yes. Leading a school chorus...?" Katie shook her head. "But I promise I'll give it my best shot."

Clint's brow furrowed as he thought it over, then he nodded and ticked directions off his fingertips. "The spring festival is Saturday night. There are twenty students in the school chorus, ages ranging from five to twelve, and Melody will assist you. Practice is in the choral suite after school every day this week from five thirty to seven thirty."

Twenty kids under her supervision for ten hours? Katie shivered. Oh, jeez. Was she crazy?

She shrugged through the terror. "Piece of cake."

Matthew stopped crying and faced her slowly, an angry frown appearing. "You can't do it."

Katie forced a smile. "Why not? The school needs someone to lead the chorus and I'm here and willing."

Matthew dragged his forearm over his wet cheeks and sniffed. His frown deepened. "You don't know what to do."

"I know how to read music and play piano." She glanced at Clint and tried to brighten her faltering smile. "I have experience. I sang in high sch—"

"But there'll be kids," Matthew snapped. "You don't like kids."

"Yes, I do." Katie leveled a stern gaze at Matthew. "Of course I like k—"

"You don't even know how to babysit," Matthew said. "Yesterday, when you were supposed to be watching us, you let Rascal jump on the table and get carrots everywhere, you couldn't change Sophia's diaper and you lost the triplets." He raised his eyebrows as he looked at the principal. "She was gone forever looking for them. Me and Emma coulda died while she was gone and she wouldn't have even known it."

Katie's mouth fell open. She clamped it shut, faced Clint and held up a finger. "First of all, I did babysit six kids yesterday and the…uh…carrot part is true. But," she stressed, "Landon's dog is as big as some small horses so I wouldn't be the only one that would have trouble pulling Rascal off a table. And even though it was my first time changing a diaper, I managed to change my niece's after three—no, four tries."

Or was it five?

Thinking, Katie glanced at the ceiling then refocused on Clint. "Yes, four. It was definitely four tries. And I also managed to catch two of the triplets in the front yard less than three minutes after they managed to get the front door open and take off. Which—" she waved her hand in the air "—I tell you, was a feat in itself because those two boys are as fast as jackrabbits and took pleasure in watching me struggle. As for Matthew and Emma dying while I was outside for three minutes—" she cut her eyes at Matthew "—there wasn't much chance of that since they were sitting safely on the living room floor, glued to *Goblins of War*—which I took the time to set up for them."

Clint eased farther back in his chair and clicked the push button on his ballpoint pen. "*Goblins of War*?"

Katie nodded. "It's a video game."

Matthew sprang to his feet. "With lots of blood in it,

and she let Emma play it, too, so she'll probably have nightm—"

"Matthew, that's enough." Mouth trembling, Katie stood. "I mean it." She firmed her voice on her next words, even though her insides still quivered. "You've been taught better than to argue with adults or rip signs down, no matter how angry or sad you may be. Go have a seat outside and wait for me there while I speak with Mr. Waterson in private."

Matthew glared up at her then moved to speak.

"Now," Katie said, pointing toward the door.

Matthew held her steady gaze for a moment then trudged to the door.

After he left, Katie faced Clint and sighed. "I'm sorry about that. Landon has told me Matthew is normally very well behaved. He's just been through so much lately…" She shook her head. "He's angry with me and he was right about me being new to this kind of thing. I haven't spent much time with him or his sisters and now that I think about it, I probably shouldn't have let Emma play such a violent video game. So that won't happen again." She lifted her chin. "But I'm a fast learner and I promise I would never do anything to jeopardize any of the children's safety."

Clint remained quiet, clicking the push button on the pen several times, then leaned forward and propped his elbows on the desk. "Watching kids can be stressful no matter how much experience someone might have. Are you sure you want to take this on?"

Katie swallowed hard. Did she want to force her way into Matthew's life by arguing with him? Definitely not. What she wanted was for him to be happy again. And right now, leading the school choir was the best chance she had of securing an opportunity to win his trust.

"It's not a matter of want," she said quietly. "It's a matter of need. I need to do this for Matthew since his mother can't. So he can learn to trust me and, hopefully, find a way through his grief."

A kind light entered Clint's eyes. "All right. The first practice begins tonight at five thirty. As I said, Melody will assist you and I'll attend the first couple of practices just to make sure everything's well in hand."

"Thank you. Is it okay if I take Matthew home for the rest of the school day and help him cool off before the first practice? I'd like to try to get him in a better frame of mind before we start, if I can."

"That'd be fine, and I look forward to seeing you both again this afternoon."

"I'll be back with Matthew and Emma at five thirty sharp." Katie shook his hand, thanked him again and left.

Surprisingly, Matthew had obeyed her for once. He had sat in the chair beside Heath outside the principal's office and waited for her return.

"Let's go. I'm taking you home for a while to cool off." She motioned for Matthew to follow her and smiled at the little boy still waiting for his turn with the principal. "Goodbye, Heath. I hope your day gets better."

Despite the worried shadows in his eyes, Heath smiled and waved goodbye.

Finally, a break. Maybe Heath would be one of the kids attending choir practice. That way there'd be one more familiar face in the crowd.

Once they made it outside, Katie led the way across

the parking lot to the car. Matthew followed slowly and made no move to enter the car when they reached it.

"Is Mr. Waterson still letting you lead the choir?" he asked, scowling.

"Yes. Our first practice is this afternoon, and you, me and Emma are all going." Katie opened the driver's-side door then paused, meeting Matthew's stare over the hood of the car. "I don't know what to say to you. I was *so* embarrassed back there."

"Good," he said, his tone hard but his chin wobbling. "I don't want you to do it. Even Uncle Landon would be better at it than you, and he doesn't even play the piano."

"I know you'd prefer Landon." Legs shaking, Katie jingled her keys and shifted from one foot to the other. "And knowing Landon, he probably would be better at it than me. He's better at taking care of you, Emma and Sophia. Better at knowing what to do in situations like this. And you know who else was better than me?"

Oh, God. She should stop talking, she really should. But that sad, empty feeling deep inside her had become so strong it made her ache to the point that she could barely draw a decent breath.

"Your mom," Katie said. "Jennifer was better at everything. She was a wonderful mother and she'd know exactly what to do right now when I don't. I'd never try to take her place—I never could. But she was my only sister and I miss her just as much as you do. I loved her as much as—" She looked away and watched the traffic pass along the nearby highway, cringing as a hot tear rolled down her cheek. "I loved her as much as I love you whether you choose to believe that or not. I want to do this for you—and for *her*—because I know she would've wanted to hear you sing at that festival. So can we please, just this once, call a truce?"

He didn't answer. The silence continued for what seemed like forever and the only sounds were the speeding cars in the distance, but then…

"Okay."

Katie faced him, wiped the tear from her cheek and raised her brows. "Okay?"

Eyes suspiciously wet, Matthew nodded as he opened the passenger door.

"Matthew?" She waited until he stopped and looked at her. "It's been a bad day for both of us. Do you remember what your mom used to say always fixed a bad day?"

Hesitating, he said, "Ice cream."

Katie grinned. "It might not be the best thing for me to do in this situation but I say we take your mom's advice and go for a rocky road cone on the way back to Landon's. Might help us both feel better. That okay with you?"

Matthew watched her for a moment then a tiny but honest-to-goodness smile appeared. "Yes, ma'am. Thank you."

Katie smiled back, and the painful ache inside her faded just a tad.

Landon rubbed Sophia's back and paced the nursery, humming softly, until her breathing grew deep and even. When he was sure she was asleep, he laid her in the crib and smoothed his thumb over her soft curls.

Man, she was cute. Between inheriting Jennifer's curls, Frank's dimples and both of their cheerful demeanors, Sophia was as close to a perfect baby as he'd ever seen. And Emma possessed the same happy outlook as Sophia, making it easy to connect with her, as well.

If only Matthew had inherited Jennifer's and Frank's inclination to search for the positive in negative situations, Katie might have an easier time reaching him.

Landon kissed Sophia's forehead then walked to the window. The horses roamed about the paddock beneath the late-morning sunlight, a light breeze ruffled the wildflowers sprinkled across the green grass and the grounds were peaceful.

Normally, he'd clip the baby monitor to his belt and use Sophia's nap time to spiffy up the landscape or mend a fence or two. But at the moment, all he could manage to do was stare at the empty driveway and wait for Katie's sporty car to appear.

She'd left to pick Matthew up two hours ago. Surely she should be back by now.

He tugged his cell phone from his pocket and reread her last text message.

Everything's fine. We'll be back soon.

We'll be back soon? What had happened? Had Matthew gotten in trouble? Or hurt? Was that what she'd meant by *we'll* be back soon?

Good Lord, worrying accompanied this dad gig more than he'd anticipated. He dragged a hand over his face, grabbed the baby monitor and left the room. At the sound of an engine, his steps paused then sped up.

He waited on the porch as Katie's car rumbled over the hill then stopped at the end of the driveway. A cloud of dust settled around it and the doors opened. Both Katie and Matthew emerged, holding ice-cream cones.

"After you finish eating," Katie said as they climbed the front porch steps, "I'd like you to lie down for a while so you'll be refreshed for this afternoon."

"Yes, ma'am."

Landon frowned when they reached the top step. "Are you all right, Matthew?"

Matthew nodded as he passed and—*dear God*—did he actually…smile?

Landon blinked hard and watched Matthew walk inside, licking his ice cream and looking a little less angry. He turned back to Katie. "What hap—"

"Shh." Her finger smooshed against his lips and, brown eyes wide with excitement, she nudged him backward inside the house. "I'm going to tell you everything." She peeked into the kitchen where Matthew sat to finish his ice cream, placed her ice-cream cone on the table by the door then shoved Landon farther down the hall. "We just have to find somewhere private." Her hair brushed his cheek as she glanced around then focused over his left shoulder. "Back here."

Landon stumbled as she pulled him through his bedroom, into his bathroom and shut the door.

"He smiled." She clapped her hands and started that bounce of hers again. The kind that drew his attention to the tempting parts of her he tried to be a gentleman and ignore. "He actually smiled. You saw it, too, didn't you?"

Stepping back, he looked down at the tile beneath his boots. "Yeah." The light fixture over the sink. "I was pleasantly surpri—"

Something brushed the top of his head then dangled over his face. It was pink. Skimpy. And had that damned delicious scent Katie sported.

He tugged it down and it fell into his palm, the silk against his skin stirring latent urges in other parts of his body as he spun around and eyed the shower rod above him. Bras—at least a dozen of them—sprawled over the metal pole, the loose straps swinging flirtatiously at the brush of his shoulder.

"Oh, I forgot about those." Katie stopped bouncing. "They should be dry by now. I'll get them out of here when we finish talking." She gripped his shoulders, her eyes bright. "Matthew smiled at school, too. Not at first when I volunteered, but afterward when I brought him home to cool off and offered to get him ice cream. Well, I know most kids would smile at leaving school and getting ice cream, but that doesn't matter as much right now. All that matters is that… He. Smiled."

Landon admired the attractive flush in her cheeks for a moment, before asking, "Wait, you volunteered for what?"

"To lead the school chorus in the spring festival." She firmed her grip on him and moved closer. "I know what you're thinking because I thought it myself. I've never done something like this before and there are twenty kids and—"

"Twenty?"

"Yes." She winced. "And the festival's this weekend, so I have to practice with them every afternoon this week. But I can do it. I *will* do it. For Matthew." Her smile fell. "He tore up the posters about the festival at school. That's why the principal wanted one of us to come. And when I asked Matthew why he did it, he said it was because Jennifer was supposed to be here to lead the chorus and that she'd promised to sing a duet with him."

Landon closed his eyes briefly, his stomach dropping. "Man."

"I know, right?" Katie squeezed his shoulders. "He's so angry and sad. I couldn't bring myself to let things end like that. To leave him with the memory that she wasn't there for something he was looking so forward to. I know it won't be the same—that I'm no substitute for Jennifer—but I can be there for him in my own way. I can help make Saturday night a little less sad, at least. Give him a good memory to go with the bad. And he smiled because of you. Because you told me to use my heart instead of my head and that's exactly what I did today." She paused to catch her breath. "So, what do you think?"

The eager excitement in her dark eyes and soft smile kicked him right in the chest.

"I think he'll love having you there." He smiled. "And I think you just took your first step toward being a fantastic aunt. Sophia and I will be happy to chauffer you, Matthew and Emma to every practice."

She beamed. "The first one's today at five thirty."

"Okay, but…" Something caught his eye across the room. He pointed at a beige ball sitting on one the medicine shelves above the sink. "What is that?"

She glanced over her shoulder, faced him again and smiled. "A bath bomb."

"A what?"

"Bubble bath in a solid form. Sandra's Sexy Suds?

It's the brand I'm working on and, believe it or not, you helped me solve one of those problems, too. You inspired the title for that one."

Oh, Lord. Bras *and* bubble baths?

"No." Firming his voice, he repeated, "No, no, no. I want that out of here. And these, too." He held up the bra in his hand, face heating when he realized he was rubbing the material with his fingertips. He dropped it back to his side. "I want it all out of here."

She frowned. "The bras were only for today, but I'd like to keep the bath bombs in here, if I could?"

He shook his head. "Nope."

"Please?" She tilted her head at an adorable angle. "They get cracked in my overnight bag and crumble, and there's no place to put them in the guest bathroom since all of the kids' stuff is in there. It's just one shelf. You have three more above it to put your stuff on."

Man, she was gorgeous. Those big brown eyes, long hair and pouty mouth made even his toes tingle. So much so, he couldn't bring himself to refuse her.

"All right," he forced out. "But just one shelf."

"Thank you, Landon. Thank you, thank you, thank you. Oh, I could just…" She stared at him, mouth opening then closing as she stepped forward then back. "I could just kiss you again."

And she did, bouncing right into his arms, planting her lips against his and searing him through all the way to the thick heels of his boots.

He should've put a stop to it. Should've pulled away and referenced decorum, but the taste of her and the feel of her pulled him in and coaxed his arms around her. Her sweet taste hit his tongue, her soft curves filled his hard planes, her delectable scent surrounded him and he was lost.

Her silky bras, dangling from overhead, brushed the bare skin of his neck and the vision he conjured up of her reclined in his tub with only scintillating bath bubbles covering the sexiest parts of her body spurred him on. He angled his head and deepened the kiss, absorbing her moan of pleasure and relishing the feel of her eager palms as they roamed over his back and buttocks.

He groaned, reached for her soft hips and gripped— empty air.

Breathing hard, he dragged his eyes open and struggled to focus on her face.

She stood a couple feet away, her hands up in the surrender position, long hair mussed and that beautiful mouth soft and open. She moved to speak once. Twice. And by the third try, she still hadn't managed to make a sound.

It took everything he had not to pick her up, carry her to his bed and make love to her for at least a month.

He cleared the husky feeling from his throat. "Are we through talking now?"

Expression stunned, she nodded slowly as her attention drifted down his body.

"Good." He thrust the bra he held toward her and, when she took it, slipped past her, opened the bathroom door and hauled ass before he could change his mind.

Chapter 6

Good gracious, Landon's kiss could set a girl's soul on fire.

Katie secured her seat belt, stared out the window of Landon's truck at an empty paddock and tried to focus on how to handle her first chorus practice rather than how much she'd enjoyed that sexier-than-all-get-out smooch from Landon six hours ago.

Oh, but that was a difficult thing to do when her lips still tingled from the memory of his persuasive kiss. And belly flips—good Lord! Despite the long afternoon filled with ranch work and babysitting, her stomach had somersaulted every time Landon's charismatic presence drew near. The only moments of peace she'd experienced had been when she'd driven into town alone to pick Emma up from school two hours ago.

"Comfortable, baby?"

Katie started, all her senses springing to life as Landon's deep drawl filled the extended cab. She twisted around and gazed longingly toward the back seat, about to answer him, when she noticed Landon smiling down at Sophia, who cooed in her car seat.

Katie's stomach dropped. Great. Just great. Here she was getting these delicious shivers over Landon's huskily voiced concern and it turned out he was talking to a six-month-old.

She clamped her mouth shut, faced forward again and frowned. And what was up with that icky sensation knotting in her middle? Was it disappointment? Or…jealousy, maybe?

"Oh, no," she mumbled under her breath.

Fawning all over Landon and kissing him twice was bad enough, but allowing her misguided libido to become jealous over him? And, with all people, a six-month-old? Never!

She clutched her belly and whispered sternly to herself, "Stop it. Focus on the kids and stay out of Landon trouble."

The driver's-side door opened and Landon got in the truck. He cranked the engine then paused and studied her face. "You all right?"

Face flaming, Katie stared back at him. "I—I'm fine. Why do you ask?"

Expression concerned, he gestured toward her middle. "You're holding your belly like you're about to be sick."

She placed her palms flat on her denim-clad thighs. "Nope. I'm fine."

A foot kicked the back of Katie's seat and Katie

glanced back at Emma. "Are you nervous about chorus practice, Aunt Katie?"

"Nope. Not at all." Katie shook her head and forced a smile, though she had to admit the thought of leading the first chorus practice had definitely contributed to her overall discomfort. "I'm looking forward to singing with you and Matthew."

And she really was, even despite the idea of spending two hours with twenty rambunctious children and struggling to combat her growing attraction to Landon.

"Aren't you excited about singing?" Katie asked Emma.

Emma smiled. "Yep."

"How about you, Matthew?" Katie looked over her left shoulder at Matthew, who'd just climbed in the truck, sat beside Sophia's car seat and shut the door.

Matthew shrugged. "I guess."

"Can you turn the radio on so we can sing on the way, Aunt Katie?" Emma piped from the other side of Sophia as Landon drove up the driveway.

"Sure." Katie studied Landon's dashboard—good grief, there were a thousand buttons—and tried not to dwell on the lack of pep in Matthew's monotonous tone. No worries, she reassured herself. After their arguments in the principal's office and school parking lot this morning, Matthew had actually thawed a bit and cracked a smile. That one smile alone would help her manage to stand up in front of a small crowd of unfamiliar, and possibly unruly, kids.

"It's up here," Landon said, tapping a preprogrammed button on a touch screen in the center of the dash.

Moments later, upbeat kids' music filled the cab's

interior and Emma started singing off-key with the lyrics. Matthew groaned and covered his ears.

Landon looked in the rearview mirror and joined Emma's off-key singing. When Matthew laughed, Landon stopped singing and smiled. His tanned cheeks and the faint lines on both sides of his sensual mouth only enhanced his magnetic appeal.

Boy, he was handsome.

"A preprogrammed kids' station," Katie teased over the music. "Y'all do this often?"

"Occasionally." Landon winked at her.

Mercy. Katie cleared her throat. "Thank you for driving us to the school tonight." She waved a hand toward the dashboard. "It was dark the last time I caught a ride with you. I didn't appreciate how nice of a truck this is."

Smile widening, he patted the steering wheel as he drove. "V8 engine, shift-on-the-fly capability, trailer sway control, all-terrain tires, heated seats and mirrors, drop-in bedliner, satellite radio and…" He jerked his chin upward. "A twin-panel moonroof."

Landon pressed a button and the sunshade slid back, then he pressed a second button and the large glass panel above them slid open, allowing a gentle rush of warm spring air to flood the cab and swirl the scent of honeysuckle around them.

A wistful note entered Landon's voice as he murmured, "God, I love a moonroof."

When he met her eyes, Katie raised an eyebrow. "Wow. A man's love for his truck." She shook her head slowly. "It's a thing to behold."

Landon laughed. "It's my one luxury, and it's been a lifesaver on the job on more than one occasion." His bright smile dimmed. "I'm trading it in next month for something less fancy."

Katie frowned, missing his sexy grin already. "Why?"

He looked in the rearview mirror. "For them. Matthew, especially." He lowered his voice as he continued, Emma's exuberant singing almost drowning out his words. "If I play my cards right, I'll walk away with a decent but older truck, and a stack of cash to start a college fund for Matthew. Eight years will pass before he knows it, and I want him to have a head start."

"Oh." Her heart warmed for this big, beautiful man willing to sacrifice anything for three kids he loved like his own. Katie blinked away the moisture lining her lashes and hesitated before asking, "You're planning that far ahead already? Before they're fully settled? Before I even know if…"

She bit the inside of her cheek as the guilt associated with leaving the kids returned. Only this time, the thought of returning to California and leaving Matthew, Emma and Sophia behind hit harder than it had before. Was that how she would let it play out? Could she actually bring herself to pack up next week, fly back to her old life and leave the kids to settle in with Landon?

Landon's jaw clenched, then he smiled. Or at least, he tried to smile. His tight grin looked as insincere to her as the one she struggled to pin on her face felt.

"No matter where Matthew is in eight years," Landon said, "if he decides to go to college, he'll need the money. Every penny will help."

Katie focused on the road in front of them.

Landon glanced toward the back seat. "Guys, you

aren't getting too much wind back there, are you? You okay with the moonroof being open?"

Emma stopped singing long enough to answer, "Yes, sir."

Matthew, still covering his ears and looking annoyed, nodded.

Landon's smile renewed and he returned his attention to Katie. "Ready to lead your first music lesson?"

Katie twisted her hands in her lap. Was she? At this point, she guessed she'd have to be. There wasn't much of a choice. "I suppose."

Landon glanced at the kids in the back seat then leaned so close, Katie could feel the heat emanating from his broad chest and smell the light scent of his aftershave. "I can stay, you know? I'll drop you and the kids off at the front of the school then Sophia and I will come in and keep you company in case you need an extra hand."

And have Landon witness her first blundering attempts at leading a kids' chorus? No, thank you.

"That's not necessary," she said.

But, gracious, Landon smelled good. And he was back to being that charming, considerate man she couldn't help wanting.

Katie sat back before that starry-eyed, crazy-for-Landon side of her caused her to do something stupid like fall in his lap, trail kisses over his rock-hard abs and beg him to put his hands on her. "The secretary, Melody, will be there to help me every night, and the principal said he'd drop in for the first two practices to make sure things go well," she said, her breath catching slightly. "Plus I'm sure a parent or two will hang around."

He shrugged. "Still, it wouldn't hurt for me to stay."

Katie narrowed her eyes and leaned closer, her desire to plant another kiss on Landon momentarily forgotten as she whispered, "You're afraid I'm gonna screw up, aren't you?"

He blinked, looked away then met her eyes again. "No. That's not what I'm saying. I'm just offering my assistance."

Lips twisting, Katie nodded. "Yeah. So you can keep me from screwing up."

Landon held up a hand. "I didn't say that."

"You didn't have to."

"I only meant—"

"Are y'all fussing?" Matthew called out from the back seat.

Katie stopped talking, and so did Landon. She returned his stare, and the red flush stamping his lean cheeks eased her discomfort a bit. At least this time, she hadn't been the only one to let their temper get ahold of them. And she'd caught Landon telling a fib—possibly his first ever, she'd be willing to bet. Obviously, he had zero confidence in her abilities with the kids.

"Nope," Katie said, settling back in her seat and flashing a smile at Landon. "Not at all."

Landon grunted, shifted gears then turned off onto a steep dirt road. "We'll take a shortcut."

Clouds of dust billowed up around the truck until Landon turned onto a paved road that curved over the mountain range ahead. The bright afternoon sun warmed the rugged, green peaks that sprawled in the distance. Dense patches of wildflowers spotted the fields lining both sides of the road, adding pink, blue and purple hues to the landscape, and a swift breeze parted the slim branches of cherry trees, heavy with pink and white blooms.

The engine growled as the truck accelerated up the mountain. A rush of sweetly scented wind surged through the moonroof, tousling Katie's hair and tickling her neck. Matthew's scowl softened as he peered out the window, Sophia babbled and Emma's joyful vocals pitched higher.

Spring hadn't just sprung in Elk Valley—it was about to burst wide open. And the small, quiet valley had never looked as beautiful to Katie as it did in this moment with her nieces and nephew near her.

Laughing, she threw her arms up and wiggled her fingers in the swift currents flowing across the open moonroof. The sudden dip of the truck as it descended from the top of a mountain slope, twisting along the sharp curves, evoked a pleasant flutter in her belly. She glanced at Landon and his handsome smile kicked her heart rate up a notch, making it thump strongly in her chest.

Landon handled the next curve with precision, glanced her way and winked again. "Moonroof, baby."

Katie's breath stuck in her lungs for a moment. Oh, that "baby" rolling off Landon's tongue was most definitely for her this time, and the hot, melting sensation spreading through her body was a sign that this attraction she had for Landon was intensifying despite her efforts to stop it.

It was beyond difficult to pry her attention away from Landon and focus on the impending chorus practice, but as they drew closer to Elk Valley Elementary, Katie's nervous tension took over. Her shoulders stiffened when Landon turned into the parking lot and parked close to the front entrance.

"We're here," Emma announced, bouncing in her booster seat.

"Give me a sec to grab Sophia's stroller and I'll walk with you," Landon said as he opened his door.

Katie grabbed his arm, halting his movements, and whispered, "I told you I can pull this off by myself." Well, she was about 90 percent sure she could. "I don't need a chaperone."

"I'm not chaperoning." Landon smiled. A bit too innocently. "I'm being a gentleman and escorting you to the door. Then I'm gonna take Sophia for a walk around the track behind the school."

Katie frowned. "Why?"

"Because it's a beautiful afternoon, Sophia loves riding in her stroller and I think she'll appreciate a change of scenery."

The back door slammed. Matthew had hopped out of the car and stood outside the truck, fidgeting impatiently.

"Okay." Katie tightened her grip on his arm—good golly, his biceps were like concrete—and asked, "But you're not coming in, right?"

"No." Lips twitching, he glanced down where her fingers still explored his biceps then raised an eyebrow. "Can I have my arm back now?"

"Oh." Whoops. "Sorry." She released him, unsnapped her seat belt then hopped out of the truck before he noticed her flaming face.

Katie opened the door for Emma while Landon un-

loaded the stroller and placed Sophia in it, then they
made their way toward the front entrance. Matthew and
Emma walked ahead and Landon matched his stride to
Katie's as he pushed Sophia in the stroller.

"Good turnout," Landon said. "Looks like you might
have more than twenty kids."

A small tic started at the corner of Katie's left eye.
"How…wonderful."

Small groups of parents and kids were strolling
across the parking lot and entering the school. Six boys
and two girls hurled a football back and forth on a patch
of grass between the sidewalk and the entrance, and a
trio of women huddled together a few feet away from
the kids, laughing.

"Oh, no." Katie ran her gaze over each of the three
women—one redhead, one brunette and a blonde—just
as all three glanced her way.

Landon frowned. "What?"

Before Katie could answer, a squeal erupted from
the trio.

"Katie Richards!" the blonde shouted, a gleeful expression lighting her face. "What are *you* doing here?"

Forcing a smile, Katie murmured out of the side of
her mouth to Landon, "Poppy Hadden, Carrie Williams
and Sallie Ann Marsh." Elk Valley's most prominent
gossip hounds. "That's what."

And judging from the hungry curiosity glowing on
all three of their faces as they stared at Landon and
Katie, the three women hadn't changed a bit since high
school.

A pained groan left her. "Do we have to go over
there?"

Landon glanced at Katie's face, grinned then steered her in that direction. "It'd be rude not to."

They made their way over to the women. Emma and Matthew ran off and joined the kids playing football, and Landon drew the stroller to a stop beside Katie.

"Hi, Landon," Poppy said, smiling. "It's good to see you."

"Real good," Sallie Ann echoed, her gaze drifting over Landon.

"Mmm-hmm." Carrie, blushing, waggled her fingers in the air at Landon.

Clearing his throat, Landon nodded. "Ladies."

They all simpered. Katie made a mental note to add Poppy, Sallie Ann and Carrie to Landon's list of admirers.

"And it's so good to see you again, Katie." Up close, the intrigued gleam in Poppy's eyes told Katie she was in for it. Poppy sprang forward and enveloped Katie in a perfume-laden embrace. "How long has it been since we last saw each other?"

"Oh…" Katie patted Poppy's back awkwardly, her fingers tangling in Poppy's long blond curls. "About ten years, I guess."

Poppy released Katie, stepped back and pressed her French-manicured nails to her chest. "Way too long, in my opinion." Her smile fell and a sad expression crossed her face. "I was so sorry to hear about Jennifer. She was such a great person."

"Thank you," Katie said quietly.

"So how are you holding up?" Poppy raised her voice as the kids playing football behind her shouted during a tackle. "Last I heard you were still living in California."

Katie nodded. "Los Angeles."

"Are you still singing?" Sallie Ann asked, a friendly smile on her face. She had always been the nicest of the three women. "I heard you may have gotten a record deal."

Face burning, Katie looked at the kids playing football and shook her head. "Nah, I gave up singing."

Sallie Ann frowned. "But why? You were so good."

"It wasn't a practical career choice, I guess." Katie winced as three of the boys screamed and tackled another boy, falling into a pile on top of him.

Oh, dear Lord, she hoped none of those boys were in the choir.

Poppy glanced over her shoulder at the kids. "Tone it down, boys. You're scaring people."

Katie pointed at the kids. "Are one of those boys yours?"

"One?" Poppy scoffed. "Try six."

"Six?" Katie asked.

"Three sets of twin boys," Poppy said. "You remember Lenny Drigger?"

Katie nodded. Lenny had been handsome, a bit wild and had liked women. A lot.

"I married him nine years ago," Poppy continued. "Now, I have over half a dozen males in my house on a daily basis. Don't get me wrong, I love every one of my boys, but six kids can be a chore. I swear, that man's not going to touch me again till after I go through menopause."

A strangled sound emerged from Landon. Cheeks red, he ducked his head and dragged a hand over the back of his neck. "I'm gonna take Sophia for her walk now."

"Oh, now don't run off, Landon," Poppy said, stepping forward and smiling down at Sophia. "We all heard you'd taken Frank's children in. That was so wonderful of you." She looked at Katie. "Is that why you're back in Elk Valley now? To visit the kids?"

Katie put her shoulders back and lifted her chin. "Yes. As a matter of fact, Landon and I are both taking care of the kids for a couple of weeks and I'm leading the choir practice tonight."

Poppy blinked. Sallie Ann and Carrie looked, open-mouthed, from Katie to Landon then back.

"You and Landon?" Carrie asked. "You two are together?"

"Nope."

"No."

Katie and Landon spoke at the same time. Though it was the truth, Landon's denial sent an uncomfortable pang through Katie.

She glanced up at him and rolled her shoulders, trying to shake off the strange disappointment. "We're just helping each other out with the kids, you know?" Katie turned back to Poppy. "And he's been kind enough to let me stay at his place."

Poppy's eyes widened. "You've moved in with Landon?"

"No, she's just using the guest room for a couple weeks." Landon checked his watch and looked at Katie. "It's almost time for practice to start, so I'm gonna take Sophia for her walk now and let you get to it. I'll stop by my sister's café and get us some takeout before I swing back by and pick you and the kids up. That'll give you one less thing to worry about. You want anything in particular?"

Katie shook her head. "No. Anything'll be fine. Thank you."

"I'll be back in two hours. I'll have my cell on me if you need anything." Landon waved to the other women. "Nice seeing you, ladies."

Katie watched as Landon said goodbye to Matthew and Emma, turned the stroller around and started walking down the sidewalk. Something about the children's exuberant shouts as they played and the sight of Landon's broad back moving farther and farther away made Katie's hands shake, and she wondered how she'd ever thought she could handle this on her own.

"Landon?"

He stopped and glanced over his shoulder. Her fear must've shown in her expression because he smiled and, voice gentle, said, "You're gonna do great."

She managed to smile back and that act alone made her feel a great deal more capable.

"Wow." Poppy stared after Landon, her gaze full of admiration. "Landon drops you and the kids off, babysits the baby, picks you up and brings takeout for dinner? A man doesn't do those kinds of things if he's not into you, Katie."

"It's not like that," Katie said. "He loves Sophia, Emma and Matthew. He's doing it for them."

Though it wasn't an unpleasant thought to imagine Landon doing all of this for her. As a matter of fact, it was a really good thought. But the last thing she or Landon needed right now were rumors of romance between the two of them—good Lord, her mother would declare her a jezebel. And by no means did she want to make Landon feel uncomfortable or as though he were obligated to provide more than just coparenting assistance to her.

No, she needed to keep her focus on what was important—the kids. So, from this point forward, she would no longer fixate on Landon, kiss or grope him. And she'd be extra careful not to fuel any inaccurate romance rumors.

"There is absolutely nothing going on between me and Landon," Katie stressed. "We're just parenting together temporarily for the kids."

"Well, whatever Landon's reasons," Poppy said, "he's a great guy."

"Yeah." That, Katie definitely agreed with. "He's the best."

A football whizzed by and smacked into Poppy's elbow. Sallie Ann and Carrie jumped.

"All right, this football game is over," Poppy said, snatching up the football and heading for the parking lot. "Tommy and Teddy, get over here now." She smiled over her shoulder at Katie. "My other four boys are yours for two hours."

"Four?" Katie asked, cringing as four of the loudest boys from the football game ran inside the school.

"And our little girls," Sallie Ann said, patting Katie's arm as she and Carrie walked away.

After they left, Katie walked toward the school entrance. The chatter and laughter of kids grew stronger with every step, and that 90 percent certainty she'd had earlier about being able to handle them dwindled down to something closer to 10 percent.

* * *

"If you look at your watch one more time, I'm going to kick you out of my café."

Landon, seated at a bar stool, tore his gaze away from his wristwatch and glanced up. He made a face at Amber, who stood on the other side of the bar. "You'd do that to your own brother?"

"No doubt." Amber tossed a blond curl over her shoulder and grinned. "I've been speaking to you for the past five minutes and I don't think you've heard a word I've said." She gestured toward the small car seat on the counter. "And poor Sophia has been begging for your attention since you came in. I bet she's beginning to feel neglected."

As if in agreement, Sophia cooed up at him from her car seat as she kicked her feet and pumped her fists.

After escaping nosy Poppy, Sallie Ann and Carrie by taking Sophia for a walk around the school track for half an hour, Landon had driven over to Amber's café and placed an order for to-go burgers and fries for supper. Matthew and Katie had had a tumultuous day and Emma wasn't used to spending an extra two hours at school in the afternoon. He figured Katie and the kids would be tired, hungry and ready to crash by the time he picked them up, and he'd looked forward to visiting Amber.

But ever since he walked away from Katie an hour and a half ago, he hadn't been able to think of anything except how Katie was faring at her first choir practice.

Landon smiled, leaned down and kissed Sophia's forehead. "Sorry, baby."

"You gonna give Katie one of those, too?" Amber asked.

Landon jerked upright and searched his sister's blank expression. "Give her what? A kiss?"

God knows he'd given Katie a rather racy one earlier today in the bathroom, of all places. If she hadn't broken away and if he hadn't managed to control himself, they'd have probably ended up in his bed. Then there was that kiss at Katie's motel room the other night, though that one hadn't been his fault. That kiss had been all Katie.

Beautiful, impulsive and sweetly passionate Katie...

"I meant an apology," Amber said. "You know, for doubting her ability to lead a choir practice? That's why you've been checking your watch every two minutes for the past half hour, right?" She propped her elbows on the bar and studied his face. "Is there something going on between you two I should know about?"

Landon forced a laugh and dragged a hand through his hair. "What?" He puffed out a heavy breath. "No."

Amber grinned. "Oh, I think there is something going on between you two. Something romantical, maybe?"

"That's ridiculous. The only reason I've been checking my watch is because I don't want to be late picking the kids up from practice."

"And Katie, too, right?" Amber asked. "You don't want to be late picking her up either, do you?"

"Well, obviously," he said. "She comes with the kids."

Amber's brows raised, a somber expression crossing her face. "Does she?"

"You know what I mean."

"Do I?" Amber asked. "Because I can tell you from experience, a woman doesn't find it very flattering to be thought of as part of a package deal. As a matter of fact, dating or making an offer of marriage to Katie just for the sake of the kids is, in my opinion, a surefire way to let her know how much you don't care about her."

"What the hell? How'd we take this conversation from apologies and kisses to dating and marriage?" Landon glanced around the café, grateful to find the most recent couple dining had already left, and lowered his voice on his next words. "Besides, I'm not discussing my private life in the middle of downtown Elk Valley."

Poppy Hadden, Sallie Ann Marsh and Carrie Williams were probably doing enough of that already. He recalled his and Katie's earlier conversation with them and the thought of what lewd gossip they might already be spreading around town about him and Katie caused him to shudder in disgust.

"Don't cuss in front of Sophia." Amber smoothed a hand over Sophia's curls as the baby smiled then turned back to Landon. "And we're not in the middle of downtown Elk Valley—we're inside my place of business, which happens to be empty at the moment. I only brought up apologies during this conversation—not kisses. You brought that up, and *you* referenced Katie as coming 'with the kids.'"

A phrase which, Landon conceded, he knew was a sore spot with Amber. Two years ago, when Amber had told Nate he was the father of her triplets, Amber had been concerned Nate would feel obligated to stay in Elk Valley and marry her just for the sake of the babies. And she'd been equally afraid Landon would insist Nate do so, as well.

Landon squirmed on his bar stool. Amber had been right. At the time, Landon had insisted Nate own up to his responsibilities and had insisted it was Nate's duty to marry Amber. So when Nate had proposed, Amber had believed Nate was doing so solely for the babies and not because Nate truly loved her. Landon had never seen Amber so hurt, and he'd felt so ashamed for contributing to it.

"I'm sorry." Landon reached out and squeezed Amber's hand gently. "I didn't mean to dredge up bad vibes. And I really didn't mean what you thought I did. Honest to God."

Amber sighed. "Good, because I like Katie and wouldn't want to see her hurt like that. So just a word of advice from your baby sister who loves you. If you're in, you better be all in with her. And I mean *her*, apart from the kids. Otherwise, it's best to keep your distance in a romantic sense." She took his hand between both of hers and squeezed back. "I know you, Landon. You're a perfect gentleman. If you were to ever, unintentionally or not, hurt a woman in that way—especially Katie— you'd regret it for a very long time."

Landon slumped on his bar stool, a rueful smile crossing his lips. "You know I'm beginning to hate the fact that you're right all the time."

Amber laughed, and he knew all was forgiven. "I'm glad to hear you finally admit that I am."

The door to the kitchen swung open and a waitress walked over and sat two bags filled with takeout dinners on the counter. "Two cheeseburger kids' meals with

fries and hot fudge sundaes, and two double cheeseburger meals with fries and banana splits."

Amber's smile widened as she gestured toward the
rosy glow of the setting sun outside the window. "Good
thing it'll be bedtime for Matthew and Emma soon,
otherwise they'd run you and Katie ragged after all
that sugar."

Laughing, Landon stood. "Let's hope they turn in
tonight without much resistance." He slid his wallet out
of his back pocket, fished out enough bills to cover the
meals and provide a hefty tip and handed the money to
the waitress. "Thanks, Karla."

"Thank *you*, Landon." Karla smiled, her gaze roving
over him from head to toe. "Feel free to drop in anytime. I'm always happy to wait on you."

Landon's neck heated as Karla returned to the kitchen.

Amber issued a sound of amusement. "If you ever do
decide to do some serious dating, Landon, I can assure
you that you won't have to look very far for a partner."

Maybe. And Karla, like most of the women who'd
hit on him recently, was smart, hardworking and pretty.
But none of those women were Katie.

He froze. Where the hell had that come from?

Nowhere, he reassured himself. The thought had
only occurred to him because he'd spent way too much
time around women and their romantic notions about
him and Katie today.

Neck heating, Landon grabbed the bags. He asked
Amber as he headed toward the door, "Mind watching
Sophia for minute while I put these in the truck? I'll be
back in a minute."

Maybe two minutes. He needed to suck in some fresh

mountain air, collect himself and steer his thoughts in a different direction before driving back to the school to pick up Katie and the kids. Because he had no intentions of letting this flirtation with Katie get out of hand to the point that he misled her. He, like Amber, liked Katie way too much to want to risk hurting her.

Fifteen minutes later, Landon turned into the parking lot of Elk Valley Elementary and noticed several kids leaving the school hand-in-hand with their parents. It was seven thirty on the dot and practice, it seemed, had just ended.

Landon glanced in the rearview mirror at the rear facing car seat. The sun was setting behind them and a bright orange glow lit up the back of the cab. Sophia babbled and her tiny hands lifted above the car seat as she played.

"All right, Sophia," he said softly. "No matter how bad this first practice may have gone, we're gonna do our best to reassure Katie she can be successful at this if she just follows through." He waited as a woman and a little girl crossed in front of him then parked in front of the school's entrance. "We'll just smile and say, Katie…"

There she was, ten feet ahead, standing—no, *being dragged to the ground*, by Matthew and four other screaming boys on a patch of grass beside the sidewalk.

"Oh, shi—" Landon bit his tongue, glanced at Sophia in the rearview mirror again and said, "Shoot." His hand fumbled over the keys as he cut the engine and thrust his door open. "Oh, shoot." Heart slamming in his chest, he scooped Sophia out of her car seat, cradled her close to his chest and walked briskly across the parking lot, shouting, "Matthew, cut that out right now!"

The boys stayed right where they were, piled atop Katie, shouting what sounded like victory yells as she lay motionless, face-first on the ground. Emma, three men and two women—including Poppy—stood several feet away, watching and laughing. Good God, why weren't any of the adults doing anything?

Landon finally reached the writhing pile of boys. Supporting Sophia with one arm, he bent, grabbed the waistband of Matthew's jeans with his free hand and dragged him off Katie. "Cut it out, Matthew," he snapped. "What do you call yourself doing?"

Matthew rolled over, lay on his back in the grass and, breathing heavily, smiled. "Playing football."

Landon frowned. "Football?"

"Yep." The muffled assertion came from somewhere near the bottom of the stacked boys. "Play's over. Get off me."

Three of the boys laughed and one groaned good-naturedly but all four boys scrambled off Katie and darted over to Poppy.

Katie rolled over in the grass beside Matthew and, clutching a football to her chest, called out, "Five bucks, Poppy." She grinned at Landon. "The ball is still in my possession and I've earned it."

Emma ran over to Landon's side, jumped up and down and giggled. "The twins acted up at practice and Aunt Katie told them if they were good, she'd play football with them after. She made a bet that the twins couldn't get the ball and she won."

Matthew propped himself up on his elbows and

looked at Katie with something he couldn't quite read— was it pride?—in his eyes. "She's fast, Uncle Landon. We almost couldn't catch her."

Landon's frown melted away as he stared down at Katie. Grass was tangled in the dark strands of her hair, dirt streaked one of her flushed cheeks and her brown eyes were so bright with enjoyment, he couldn't help but grin back.

"You scared the devil out of me, you know that?" Landon asked, extending his free hand and pulling her to her feet. "I thought they were trying to kill you."

Katie laughed. "I knew it." Now standing, she brushed dirt off the front of her thighs and backside. "Go ahead and admit you told a fib earlier. You doubted I could pull tonight off, didn't you?"

Smiling, Landon plucked a blade of grass from her bangs. "I take that to mean practice went well?"

Katie smacked his chest playfully. "It did, but you didn't answer my question."

Landon stilled. The heat of her palm, still resting against his chest, seared right through his thin T-shirt and imprinted itself on his skin, and a gentle, wanting expression crossed her face as she met his eyes.

Sophia squealed from her perch on his left hip and patted the back of Katie's hand on his chest. Landon glanced down at her small fingers wiggling against Katie's slim wrist and there was something so unifying about the small circle they made. Something warm, comforting and...fulfilling. Something he found himself wanting more than anything.

If you're in, you better be all in with her...apart from the kids.

Landon shifted closer to Katie. "I'm sorry I doubted you." Drifting the backs of his fingers along her pink cheek, he whispered, "I'm glad your first practice went well."

Katie's grin dimmed a bit. "Thank you." She removed her hand from his chest, stepped back and, gesturing over her shoulder at Poppy, said quietly, "Wouldn't want to fuel more gossip."

She turned away, helped Matthew stand then led them toward the truck, holding Emma's hand. Landon slowly followed and waved at Poppy as she called out goodbye.

Maybe it was Jennifer's letter and Katie's insistence she hadn't been involved in any matchmaking shenanigans on Jennifer's part. Maybe it was Amber's mention of kisses, dates and marriage earlier today. Or maybe it was the warm spring breeze and sound of children's laughter in the air. Whatever prompted it, Landon found himself wondering what life might be like if Katie stayed in Elk Valley—not just with the kids…but with him, as well.

It also made him wonder what life would be like if she chose to leave instead…and take the kids with her.

Chapter 7

"She's a natural with kids, I tell you." Clint Waterson, principal of Elk Valley Elementary, smiled at Landon. "An absolute natural."

Landon watched as Katie and the school secretary, Melody, stood in front of the stage in Elk Valley Elementary's cafeteria, waving their arms and calling out directions. Almost a dozen kids of various ages and heights milled about on the stage. Some chased each other behind the curtains, others jumped from one step to another on the small staircases on both sides and a few lay sprawled across the three-tiered choral risers in the center. Chatter, laughter and shouts echoed around the room, drowning out the sound of her voice.

Katie glanced over her shoulder and, laughing awkwardly, lifted her arms as though to say, *What's a girl to do?*

Landon smiled and raised an eyebrow. Man, she was adorable.

When he'd accepted Katie's invitation to drive her and the kids to the school, come inside with Sophia and watch tonight's practice—the final one before the spring festival tomorrow—Landon hadn't been sure what to expect, but he'd had no doubts that Katie had thrown herself wholeheartedly into the spring festival venture with Matthew and Emma. He'd hoped to find her as pleased and energetic as she had been after the first practice.

Over the past three days, he'd only seen Katie and the kids a handful of hours. She'd hit the stable each morning before dawn to muck the stalls, spent most of the day watching Sophia and working on her laptop while he worked with the horses, then drove Matthew and Emma into town at five thirty for choir practice each night. Landon had offered to continue dropping them off and picking them up from practice but Katie had politely declined. She insisted she would drive to save Landon time and keep from inconveniencing him.

Not wanting to argue the point, Landon had agreed then found himself sitting on the front porch with Sophia, watching the driveway impatiently for her sporty car to arrive. When Katie returned at eight each night, she, Matthew and Emma had been all tired smiles and excited chatter about more after-practice football games with the twins, and Landon had been lucky to get five minutes of conversation with them before all three retired to their rooms.

Though he was happy Katie was reconnecting with the kids, he couldn't help but feel left out. Forgotten, almost. But, he supposed, that was a small price to pay if it meant helping the kids reconnect with Katie. It seemed Matthew and Emma were enjoying the busy afternoons of practice and play with Katie.

And now, from the looks of things, all the kids in the room had kept Katie busy this week, too.

"A natural, you say?" Landon retrieved Sophia's fallen pacifier from her lap, returned it to her as she babbled in the stroller then glanced at Clint. "Sure you're not biased?"

"Well…" Clint shrugged, a grin appearing. "Maybe."

Landon frowned. The guy's eyes lingered on Katie a bit too much for his liking, and there was something in his tone. A hint of admiration? Approval?

"Things might've started off rocky," Clint continued, "but Katie has really taken the bull by the horns this week. She's worked wonders with the kids in a small amount of time."

No. That was more than just admiration or approval lacing his tone. There was an edge of restraint in his voice. As though he'd noticed the same appeal in Katie that Landon had, and was trying to downplay his interest.

Landon narrowed his eyes. "I thought Katie said Melody was helping her out every night. You drop in on these practices every day, too?"

Clint smiled wider. "Sure, for a little while to make sure all is well. It's my job. I wanted to check things out and make sure Katie's adjusting okay."

Yeah. Landon bet he did.

Hold up. Wincing, Landon ducked his head and studied his boots. Where had that come from? That bite of judgmental anger he'd heard in his own words? And since when had he become overprotective and... *jealous* over Katie?

He lifted his head, striving for a civil tone. "Thanks for watching out for her. How have Matthew and Emma been during the practices?"

"Better," Clint said, growing solemn. "Emma's doing well and Matthew's still quiet but he's starting to open up to Katie. I've noticed him talking and laughing more often during their duet practice." He cast Landon a sidelong look, a hesitant note in his voice. "I hear Katie's staying with you and kids while she's in town. Are the kids responding as well to her at home as they are here?"

Ah, yes. He should've guessed that was coming. After his and Katie's run-in with Poppy, Sallie Ann and Carrie at the first practice, he'd been on the receiving end of more than a few curious stares and nosy inquiries recently. Certain things in Elk Valley never changed, and the town gossip mill was obviously still in business. A man and woman in close quarters overnight added up to only one thing in most people's minds.

Even his, apparently. Since his chat with Amber and after sharing that pleasant moment with Katie outside the school after her first chorus practice, he hadn't been able to stop himself from thinking about Katie. Well, about Katie *and* him. About them raising the kids together and how different and exciting things might be if she were to stay on a permanent basis. Something Amber had been very clear in advising him against.

But there was no harm in just imagining. Not when

he had no intention of actually pursuing a permanent partnership with Katie, right?

Landon nodded. "The kids are enjoying Katie's visit and with her so close, they're warming up to her. Matthew has taken up with her a lot more since Katie started leading the choir."

Clint's smile returned as he pointed toward the stage. "All the kids are warming up to her. Even the more challenging ones."

Landon glanced at Katie. She and Melody chased a small boy—*around six, maybe?*—up a set of stairs, across the stage then back down again.

"Don't you do it, Heath," Melody said, blocking the boy's path back up the stairs. "I mean it. We eat food in the cafeteria—we don't throw it."

The boy made a face then unwrapped the candy bar in his hand. "I ain't gonna throw it. I'm too hungry."

"Could you please eat it later?" Katie asked, holding out her hand. "After we finish practice? You can't sing with food in your mouth and it would be a big help to me and Ms. Melody."

Heath looked up at the ceiling and pursed his lips. "How big of a help?"

"An immense one," Katie said.

He wiped his nose. "What's e-miss?"

"Immense." Katie shook her head. "It means big. Real big." She pointed in Landon's direction. "We have guests tonight, see? It'd be nice if we could make a good impression."

Heath considered this for a moment then sighed, slapped the candy bar in Katie's hand and darted past Melody back onto the stage.

"See?" Clint put his shoulders back. "She's a natural with kids."

"Yeah," Landon murmured.

She walked over to the piano and he studied the graceful swing of her arms by her sides, his body itching to feel her hands on him again, recalling for the millionth time just how fantastic her kisses had felt.

It was irrational of him. Not to mention irresponsible. She was the kids' aunt and a temporary guest in his house. He should heed Amber's warning and not entertain those kinds of thoughts or feelings. But no matter how much of a complication it might pose, he found himself wishing Katie would kiss him again. He wanted to feel the light brush of her breath against his cheek. Wanted to touch her soft hair and trail his palms over her slim back.

The residual effects of her two kisses lingered on his lips and heated his blood. That was the root cause of his behavior, damn it. That and those voodoo bath bubbles, casting spells of aromatic enchantment every time she used them. That was why he'd overreacted to Clint the way he had.

"Now watch this," Clint whispered, gesturing toward the piano.

Katie sat on the piano bench, leaned in then put those beautiful hands of hers on the keys. Moments later, a gentle rhythm of cheerful notes peppered the air. The chords cut through the idle chatter, stomping feet and laughter. One kid stopped running, stepped onto the riser and started singing. A few more took notice, found their places and joined the chorus. And within thirty seconds, all kids were lined up according to height on the risers, their arms still by their sides, faces lifted and happy voices filling the cafeteria.

Four kids were off-key, and two coughs and one sneeze momentarily distracted from the unity of the presentation, but it was a sight to behold.

A sound of approval escaped Landon and there he was, back to wanting Katie for his own all over again. "She's amazing."

"Told you." Clint walked off and joined Melody as she took her position in front of the chorus, leading the performance with wide sweeps of her arms.

Landon glanced down at Sophia. "Whatcha think, gorgeous? Did your aunt Katie make a splash or what?"

Sophia, eyes wide on the group of kids in front of her, made a delighted O with her mouth and kicked her arms and legs

He laughed again. "I take it you agree."

For the next two hours, the cheerful sounds of kids singing and dancing in time with Katie's music washed over the room then slowly drew to a close when night descended outside the large windows lining the wall. Parents arrived and the kids dispersed, waving goodbye and laughing. Matthew and Emma were all smiles as they bounded down the steps toward Landon.

Joyful warmth radiated throughout him at the sight.

"How'd we sound?" Matthew asked, drawing to a breathless stop.

Landon ruffled his hair and smiled. "Fantastic. Y'all are gonna do great at the festival tomorrow night. But I didn't see you and Katie practicing your duet. Is it still on?"

Matthew grinned wider, a secretive gleam in his eyes. "It's a surprise."

"Aunt Katie says it'll be stupid-us," Emma piped up, hopping in place.

Matthew scoffed. "*Stu-pen-dous.* She said our duet is going to be stupendous."

Landon stared as Matthew shook his head and laughed, the sound of it so similar to Katie's. The warmth radiating inside Landon grew as he imagined having Katie under his roof every night, laughing with the kids. Laughing with him.

But would Katie consider the idea of staying? Or, even worse, would she consider leaving with the kids?

Shaking off the chilling worry, Landon summoned a proud smile. "I believe Katie's right. Your duet will be stupendous. If it's even half as good as the whole choir's performance, the two of you are destined to be the highlight of the festival."

A little girl skipped past Landon, waving over her shoulder. "Bye, Ms. Richards."

Katie followed in her wake and waved at the students and parents filing through the exits. "See you guys at the festival tomorrow night at seven o'clock. And don't be late, I'm eager to show all of you off."

Matthew headed for the door, too. "Are we going to Aunt Amber's café now? I'm starving."

Katie tilted her head and smiled at Landon. "Sorry. I forgot to mention to you that I asked my mom to meet us at Amber's. She hasn't seen the kids this week, what with both of us juggling work and me and the kids coming to chorus practice. I thought we could meet her there for dinner and dessert on the way back home."

She blushed and glanced around at the curious looks they were receiving from nearby parents. "I mean, on the way back to your place. My mom said she was helping friends set up a booth for the festival and may not make it, but I'm hoping she will. Is that okay?"

Okay? All of it felt okay to Landon—including the slow, tender way the words *we* and *home* rolled off her tongue. Plus, the thought of sitting down and sharing a meal with her, the kids and Patricia made it feel all the more like they were becoming a family. A real one.

Landon tried to sound nonchalant. "That'd be fine."

"Yes." Matthew pumped his fist in the air and ran off.

Emma whooped and chased after him, both of them chanting in a singsong voice, "Let's go."

Silky hair brushed Landon's cheek and he turned his head to find Katie leaning close to his ear, her soft breath tickling his skin as she whispered, "Did you hear what they called me?"

Sweet heaven, she always smelled so delicious. Today, she smelled like sun-warmed honeysuckle. There was a pulse fluttering just below her jaw. He wanted to nuzzle his nose against the warm throb, breathe her in then trail open-mouth kisses down her neck to the gentle slope of her collarbone. Touch his tongue to her smooth skin.

"I…" Landon blinked hard, his attention straying to the small diamond stud in her delicate earlobe. That sensitive curve of her ear would probably feel like velvet against his thumb. "Huh?"

"Ms. Richards," Katie said. "That's what they called me. They don't see me as plain ol' Katie, that bad little girl who barely passed math or Jennifer's black sheep sister." She pressed closer, eyes bright, cheeks flushed and smile trembling. "Right here, in this little choral corner of the world, I'm known as mature, responsible Ms. Richards. Isn't it wonderful?"

Landon's mouth parted as she started that bounce of hers again. The one that preceded the gentle pressure of her embrace, the soul-searing pleasure of her lips parting his and her soft feminine sigh of satisfaction. And it had been so long since she'd kissed him.

Landon leaned in, eyes heavy and entire body *aching* for it.

Seeming to catch herself, Katie stopped bouncing and her cheeks turned bright red. She glanced around once more, patted his chest then stepped back. "Welp. I'll meet you at the truck."

She bent, kissed Sophia's cheek then hurried off, her long hair rippling across her back as she walked away.

Landon glanced at Sophia, who looked up at him and flashed a toothless grin. Scowling, he muttered something which, upon later reflection, he admitted didn't make for his finest moment.

"How come you got a kiss and I didn't?"

Katie took great pride in the fact that she'd managed to make it four whole days without smooching Landon or grabbing his butt. And there was no better way to keep her mind—and hands—off Landon's sexy backside than arguing with her mother.

"You would think a daughter who happened to be staying just twenty miles away would visit her mother at least once over the span of a week." Patricia unfolded a napkin, placed it in her lap then made that sound—

a cross between a sigh and a moan—to signify she'd been neglected. Yet again.

"I'm sorry, Mom," Katie said. "I know I should've come by to visit sooner, but I've been so busy with the kids lately that I truly haven't had much spare time."

"Well, I wish you would've made time for at least one night's stay at home." Patricia frowned. "As it is, I've been repeatedly forced to fabricate justifications to my friends for why you're living with Landon and not with me and your father. Darlene Norton just grilled me about you and Landon last night."

Good Lord. Darlene Norton, a retired schoolteacher, had prided herself on being in everybody's business and had made Katie's high school years sheer torture. From the sound of things, Mrs. Darlene was still intent upon giving her advice on how Katie led her life.

Katie glanced around Amber's café, noting the curious stares they received from a couple in a corner booth. When she'd suggested bringing the kids to meet her mother for dinner after the last spring festival practice, she'd planned to fill Patricia in on her recent success with Matthew and the school chorus. She'd hoped the café would be relatively empty so there'd be less witnesses to any head-butting that occurred. Rumors surrounding family strife were almost as popular as whispers of scandalous sex in tiny Elk Valley, and Katie had been very careful to avoid stirring up talk of either of those things over the past week.

At least Landon and the kids were on the other side of the room, talking to Amber at the bar and unable to hear her latest argument with her mother at their table.

"Mom, I'm not living with Landon in a carnal

sense—I'm visiting my nieces and nephew. You don't owe anyone an explanation. Just tell them my whereabouts are none of their business."

Patricia blinked wide eyes. "I don't speak to my friends in that way."

"Darlene Norton isn't your friend if she's pumping you for gossip. Your real friends will accept what you choose to tell them and not dig for the rest. Besides, don't I mean more to you than petty Elk Valley gossip?"

Patricia's cheeks reddened.

Katie sighed. "I know I have a tendency to embarrass you, but can we please not do this now? Landon and the kids will be back over here any minute. I have good news to share and I want us all to have a nice dinner together."

"I suppo—" Patricia stopped, her eyes widening as she looked over Katie's shoulder. "Oh, no." She smoothed a shaky hand over her topknot. "Here comes another inquisition."

Katie glanced up just as Darlene Norton stopped beside their table.

"Well, look who I've finally managed to bump into," Darlene said, a sly smile appearing as she looked Katie over. "Poppy Hadden told me you were back in town and I just asked your mother last night at canasta where you'd been hiding yourself."

Katie stifled a groan. She had a pretty good idea what all Poppy had told Darlene.

Katie smiled and glanced at her mother. "Canasta? The ladies' group still throwing down money on cards every Thursday night?" She looked at Darlene and tsked her tongue. "Didn't you fuss at me once in high school for playing poker in the cafeteria? If I recall correctly, you said gambling was crass and unladylike."

"Katie." Patricia's voice held a subtle note of censure.

Darlene adjusted the gold necklace at her throat. "Gambling is crass when it involves large sums of money, but we only play with nickels and dimes." She shrugged one slim shoulder. "There is a difference, dear."

Katie laughed. "If you say so."

She'd bet good money Darlene's so-called difference applied only to those people of whom Darlene approved.

"Poppy mentioned you were living with Landon," Darlene said. She glanced at Landon, who still stood at the bar with the kids, then turned back to Katie. "I was surprised to hear that. I wouldn't have thought you were Landon's type, though I can understand him needing a mother-type figure around for Jennifer's children."

Katie bristled. "Mrs. Norton—"

"Now, don't get offended, dear." Darlene patted Katie's shoulder. "I just meant that I thought Landon would prefer a calmer, more focused kind of woman. Someone responsible and dependable." Darlene smiled softly at Patricia. "Like dear, sweet Jennifer. We all miss her so much, Patricia."

Katie looked down and picked at her napkin. Oh, how she wanted to tell Darlene off, but…there wasn't much she could say. Jennifer had been a wonderful, dependable woman and no matter how much Katie changed, she'd never truly compare with her sister. At least, not in her mother's eyes or, she was beginning to believe, in anyone else's, either.

"Thank you, Darlene." Patricia's words were clipped.

"But I'll also thank you not to question my daughter anymore about Landon. Whatever might be going on between Katie and Landon is their business and neither you nor Poppy should concern yourselves with it."

Katie's head shot up and the stern look in her mother's eyes surprised her.

"I'm sorry, Darlene," Patricia continued, gesturing toward the table. "I don't mean to be rude, but Katie and I have some catching up to do over dinner."

Darlene, clearly disappointed at having not gleaned more gossip, waved a manicured hand and smiled. "Of course. I apologize for intruding." She glanced at Katie and, before walking away, said, "It was good to see you, Katie."

"You, too," Katie said, forcing a smile. After Darlene had left, Katie chanced a glance at her mother's red face then gulped her iced water, wincing a moment later as the cold liquid shot a pain through her head.

"I am sorry I haven't visited sooner, Mom." Katie rubbed her temples. "Not just this week—I'm sorry for not being around much the past three years, too. But right now, it's important that I continue focusing on Matthew, Emma and Sophia."

"I'm well aware of that." Patricia grabbed pink packets of sweetener from a wire holder on the table. "I just wish you would have realized that sooner."

"You mean before Jennifer messed up and designated me primary guardian?"

Patricia stopped sprinkling sweetener into her coffee cup.

"Matthew overheard you talking to Dad a few days ago," Katie added.

She looked at Matthew and Emma, who sat on bar stools at the front counter, smiling and chatting with Amber. The sight of Matthew smiling still warmed Katie's heart and made her long to wrap protective arms around him and prevent anything from ever hurting him again.

Lowering her voice, Katie continued, "Matthew heard you saying that the only reason I came back home was because Jennifer—" No. She couldn't say it out loud. Not yet. Instead, she swallowed the tight lump in her throat, turned back to her mother and asked, "Do you really believe that I don't care about them at all? Do you really think so badly of me?"

Patricia set the sweetener packets aside and met her eyes. "I'm sorry Matthew overheard me say that and I'm even more sorry he repeated it to you. I don't think badly of you, Katie, and I know you care for them. But to be honest, I never imagined you'd be interested in anything more than a short visit. I certainly didn't expect you to be interested in anything long-term."

"Well, I am interested. Very interested, as a matter of fact. It's one of the reasons I volunteered to help Matthew."

"Ah, the festival." Something odd flickered across Patricia's face. "I had an inkling that might be why you invited me to meet you today."

Katie leaned closer. Narrowed her eyes. "What's that?"

"What?" Patricia glanced down at her blouse.

"That." Katie snapped her fingers and pointed her finger at Patricia's nose. "That look on your face right now. It looks almost like…"

"Pride," a deep voice said.

Katie looked up, and there he was: said owner of sexy butt and the most skillful mouth in Tennessee.

Landon smiled. "Sorry. The kids had a longer talk with Amber than I thought they would. Hope we didn't hold you up?"

"No. Not at all." Katie waved to Sophia, who sat in the stroller Landon pushed, then motioned toward the other side of the table. "Though we might be out of room now. I wasn't sure my mom would make it but here she is."

"With bells on now that I know you're here, Landon," Patricia said, smiling. "I've missed you and the kids this past week."

His smile slipped. "Katie, too, I hope?"

Patricia nodded. "Of course. We've just been discussing that we need to spend more time together, and I told Katie that I think I know why she asked me to come today. I ran into Clint Waterson at the grocery store last night and he filled me in on Katie's volunteer efforts at the elementary school."

"You spoke to Clint about me?"

Patricia held up her hands. "I didn't ask a thing. He approached me. He thought I'd want to know what an excellent job you've done with the chorus this week. Said he'd never seen the students have so much fun. He thinks you're a natural with kids."

"He said that?" Katie couldn't stop the wide smile spreading across her face. "Clint actually said that?"

"You call the principal Clint?"

Landon was frowning at her. And was that a hint of jealousy lurking in his blue eyes? Why, yes. Yes, it was.

Katie grinned. "Yes, I call him Clint. Just like you call the school secretary Melody." She shrugged. "It's his name. And just let me bask in this praise for a sec, okay? A lot of people in Elk Valley have said a ton of things about me over the years, but no one has ever said I was a natural with kids."

"Now, that's not accurate, is it?" Patricia leveled a concerned look at Landon then stared down at her coffee, adding softly, "Jennifer said it. Maybe not in so many words, but she made her thoughts—and wishes—clear."

The ensuing silence between them grew heavy. Katie peeked at Landon beneath her lashes. The carefree light in his eyes had dimmed and his brow furrowed as he studied Sophia.

Katie stood and backed toward the front counter. "I'll go ask Amber if we can push two tables together. That way there'll be room for all of us in one place. And we really need to go ahead and order if we're going to have time to eat, get back to the ranch and let the kids get a good night's sleep for the festival tomorrow night."

Not waiting for a response, she spun around and strode to the counter. It was the coward's way out, no doubt. But she had no idea how to respond to her mom's remark because she had no idea what she was going to do. A week ago? Sure, she'd known exactly what her plan entailed. Visit Elk Valley, get to know Matthew, Emma and Sophia, let them know they could count on her whenever they needed her, then return to California, back to the status quo.

But lately, after working with Matthew at choir practice every afternoon, playing football with him and Emma, seeing their smiles more often and feeling more and more capable as an aunt…well, a little feeling inside her had blossomed. An unfamiliar but pleasant sensation that she wanted to explore.

Only, it seemed like the bigger that feeling grew, the warier Landon had begun to appear. Although his recent mood could be a result of something else entirely. Like him worrying that, given half a chance, she might jump his bones again and create an Elk Valley scandal. A concern Darlene Norton apparently shared.

Well, no sirree, she thought with a half smile. She'd promised herself days ago after her encounter with Poppy, Sallie Ann and Carrie that she'd check her impulses. No more kissing Landon and no more invading his space.

Hmm. Except maybe his bathroom. She'd definitely like to continue using his humongous bathtub.

"Can we have dessert first?" Emma asked, spinning on her bar stool when Katie reached her side. "I'm getting sprinkles, nuts, whipped cream, cherries, caramel and hot fudge on top of my ice cream."

Katie shared an amused glance with Amber. "I suppose it'll be okay just this once. But that's a lot of sugar for a tummy as small as yours. How about we narrow that down to two toppings instead?"

Emma looked disappointed then shrugged. "Okay. I'll just get whipped cream and fudge, Aunt Amber."

"Coming right up." Smiling, Amber drizzled hot fudge and added whipped cream to Emma's bowl of ice cream then placed it on a tray with three other sundaes. "Here you go, guys. Matthew ordered you, Patricia and Landon banana splits, Katie."

Matthew looked up, a shy smile crossing his face. "Do you like those, Aunt Katie?"

She smiled. "I do, thanks. That was very thoughtful of you."

He blushed. "Want me to take them to our booth?"

"That'd be great, but I underestimated how much room we'd need. Is it okay if we push a couple tables together, Amber?"

"Of course," Amber said. "Have at it."

"We'll do it," Matthew said.

Emma hopped off her bar stool, and she and Matthew carried the sundaes over to a table then started pushing a second table close.

"You're good with them."

Katie turned back to find Amber studying her and laughed. "Better than I was when I babysat for you? I'm so sorry I didn't do a better job."

"You're kidding, right?" Amber smiled. "My three rascals came home with full stomachs and tired legs. They took a three-hour nap when we got home." She laughed. "I couldn't ask for a better babysitter."

Katie blew out a breath. "Boy, that's a relief. I had a hard time keeping up with them."

"But you managed it. That's all that matters." Amber glanced across the room. "I'm not the only one who's impressed. Landon told me Matthew is looking better every day. He said you're doing a great job helping him through this, and Matthew couldn't stop telling me about the duet the two of you are doing tomorrow night at the festival. He's so excited."

Face warming, Katie rubbed the back of her neck.

"Thank you, but I can't take all the credit. Landon is the one who gave me the boost I needed to become more involved. Otherwise, I never would've been brave enough to volunteer for such an undertaking on my own. He said I've taken my first step toward being a fantastic aunt." She looked over her shoulder, her gaze clinging to Landon's muscular frame as he helped the kids set up the chairs. "He's a wonderful guy."

"He's a great brother, too," Amber said, pride in her voice. "He's helped take care of my little ones since the day they were born. You won't ever have to worry about Matthew, Emma and Sophia. Landon will take great care of them."

Katie stilled. Her eyes followed Matthew's movements as he removed each sundae from the tray and put one at every place setting. Emma, smiling, sat on her knees in a chair, tapping a spoon on the table and eyeing her ice cream. Sophia watched her siblings with wide eyes, her small feet kicking rhythmically against the stroller.

"What's the biggest difference between being an aunt and a mom?" Katie asked.

Amber paused wiping down the counter, confusion clouding her eyes. "I'm sorry?"

Katie faced her again. "How different are things when you're being an aunt as opposed to a mom?"

"In what way?"

Katie hesitated. "I don't know. Just overall, I guess."

Amber thought it over for a moment. "Well, obviously my time commitment is greater with my own children. I'm with them from sunup to sundown most days, except for the hours when I'm working. There's less sleep, more worry, the financial strain is definitely greater and nowadays, being alone for twenty minutes behind a locked bathroom door is considered a vacation." Her attention drifted off for a moment then a wistful smile appeared. "But you know what else I get more of?"

"What?"

"Love." Amber closed her eyes, hugged her arms to her chest and sighed. "So much, it spills over into every other part of my life. I can't remember what my life was like before I had them, and I wouldn't wish it any other way now." She opened her eyes. "I guess that's how it is for all parents. That's why Landon is perfect for Matthew, Emma and Sophia, you know? He's lived the bachelor life—" she cupped a hand around her grin "—and Lord knows, more than one woman around here has tried to tempt him out of it, but I think he's discovered that he's happiest with family. I've really come to believe that's why he spent so much time with my kids when they were babies. That's how I know he'll be a great dad to those three. Landon knows what he wants out of life, and they're part of that." She laughed. "Did any of that answer your question?"

Katie nodded, then forced a smile. "Yes. Thank you."

Katie left the bar and made her way to the tables Landon and the kids had arranged, studying the gentle light in his eyes when he smiled at Sophia. The happiness in his laugh when he reached over to wipe whipped cream from Emma's nose. The fondness in his gaze when he ruffled Matthew's hair.

Then she imagined Landon on his own. Without Matthew, Emma and Sophia.

And that feeling that had bloomed inside her—the happy one she'd experienced supporting Matthew and Emma, leading the chorus and wanted to explore—shrank a little more with each step she took.

Chapter 8

"Can I look now?"

Katie angled a bottle of hair spray toward the back of Emma's head. "Almost. It needs one more scoot of hair spray to be sure it holds all the way through the chorus concert. Cover your face, please."

She waited until Emma's hands shielded her eyes then sprayed her dark curls. Waving away the lingering cloud of hair product, Katie stepped back and smiled. "Now. Go to the mirror and give it a gander."

Emma lowered her hands, dashed across the guest bedroom and looked at her reflection. "It's pretty," she squealed, bouncing with excitement.

"Of course it is. You're a beautiful girl."

Emma stopped bouncing and touched her updo. Her dark eyes met Katie's in the mirror. "Do I look like Mama?"

Katie studied Emma's shiny curls gathered in a loose topknot, a few tendrils brushing her pink cheeks, then noticed the hopeful gleam in Emma's brown eyes. She swallowed hard, her own eyes brimming with tears. "Yes. You look exactly like her, and she'd be very proud of you."

Emma bit her lip then looked up toward the sky outside. "Do you think Mama will be able to hear us sing all the way up there?"

Katie waited for the knot in her throat to recede before answering. "She'll always be able to hear you, Emma—always."

Emma smiled, ran back across the room and barreled into Katie's arms. "Thanks, Aunt Katie."

Katie stumbled back, wrapped her arms around Emma and squeezed her tight. "I have to say—" she laughed, warm tears tickling her cheeks "—that's the best thank-you I've ever received for fixing someone's hair."

"Can I go show Uncle Landon?"

"Sure." Katie held up a hand as Emma darted off, her pink skirt fanning out behind her. "Just don't run. It'll mess up your…hair."

Too late. A lone curl slid out of the topknot and bounced against Emma's back before she turned the corner and jogged down the hallway.

Babbles rang out from the direction of the bed.

Smiling, Katie walked back across the room. "What're you up to, baby girl? Not getting enough attention?"

Sophia, clad in a diaper, rolled to her belly, pushed up to her hands and knees and rocked twice before lying back down. It seemed the crawling practice she and Landon had been undertaking with her was starting to do some good.

"You cute little show-off." Katie gently rolled her on her back again. "Let's get you dolled up. We've got a big night ahead."

A night she'd been looking forward to all week. Yesterday's final chorus practice had gone better than she'd expected and after they'd left Amber's café and returned to the ranch, Landon had made it a point to praise Matthew and Emma—and Katie—for doing such great work.

His words had been genuine, and he'd seemed happy enough delivering them, but she couldn't help but pick up a subtle note of disappointment in his tone. One she couldn't quite put her finger on.

That coupled with another matter had weighed so heavy on her mind, Katie had tossed and turned most of last night, toying with possible solutions and, with each new idea, hearing her mother's words repeat like a bad refrain in her head.

I certainly didn't expect you to be interested in anything long-term.

Katie grabbed the ruffled baby dress draped on the edge of the bed and slipped it over Sophia's head. "Long-term doesn't scare me as much as it used to, and it was so nice having Mom defend me for once yesterday at the café."

Once Sophia's curls cleared the collar of the dress, Katie smoothed a hand over them and studied Sophia's expression.

"How would you feel about something long-term?"

Katie asked. She slipped on Sophia's socks and rubbed her toes, watching her face. "I mean, how would you feel about coming to stay with me in California? There are great people and beautiful beaches, and so much we could do together. I've gotten pretty good at changing your diaper. I'm an ace at fixing Emma's hair and so far, I've done a decent job volunteering at the elementary school."

She held out her pointer finger, smiling as Sophia grabbed it and squeezed.

"Shouldn't I be able to do all of those things just as well on my own in California?"

Sophia cooed.

"But what if I let you down?" Katie whispered. "I used to be real good at that, you know. I failed two classes in high school. Left Elk Valley the first chance I got and rarely came back to visit my mom or your mom over the years." Her face heated. "I know I hurt them. That I wasn't as good to them as they tried to be to me."

Katie ran her thumb over Sophia's chubby cheek.

"But maybe that's just another reason why I should take you, Emma and Matthew with me. This could be my chance to take care of all of you like your mom took care of me. To protect and support you. To do my best to keep you from being scared or sad."

The look of happy adoration in Sophia's eyes made her heart skip.

"I love all three of you so much. That's what's most important no matter how many mistakes I might make, right?"

Sophia looked away, grabbed the rattle resting nearby on the bed and started babbling again.

"Yeah, I know." Katie closed her eyes, painful guilt washing over her. "Landon loves the three of you just as much as I do. And if I were to take you, what would that do to him?"

Hardwood planks in the hall floor creaked.

Katie straightened and wiped tears from her cheeks just as someone knocked on the partially opened door.

A deep, sexy drawl sounded. "Okay if I come in?" *Landon.*

"Um…" She fanned her damp face. *Stop crying. Stop it, you ninny.* "Yeah, sure."

A rush of air moved through the room as the door swept fully open and Landon's firm tread approached from behind. "Emma showed me and Matthew her new hairstyle. You did a good job."

Katie smoothed her eyebrows with shaky fingers. "It's a special night." Tucked her long hair behind her shoulders. "And a special night calls for a special updo."

"Well, it definitely made Emma's night." His voice drew closer. "She looked—"

She faced him, the skirt of her dress gliding across the front of his muscular thighs, the green silk bright against the thick denim, and her eyes locking with his.

"Beautiful," he whispered.

The low throb in his voice had nothing to do with the hairstyle she'd given Emma, and the masculine appreciation in his gaze, his clean-shaven jaw and a slight flexing of his big hands by his sides made her want to throw her arms around him again.

She refused to give in to temptation and clamped her eager hands behind her back instead. Then she twisted her fingers together. "Thank you. I think Emma looked very nice, as well."

His expression fell, his blue eyes dimming. "Is Sophia ready?"

"Yep." Her smile returned. She stepped back and swept an arm toward the bed. "Ready for inspection, sir."

Mouth twitching, his eyes roved over her from head to toe once more then he walked to the bed and lifted Sophia in his arms. "How'd Katie do, baby girl?"

Landon settled Sophia on his hip, touched the bow in her hair, checked the fit of her socks then, hesitating, tilted her bottom up and glanced at the secure fit of her diaper.

He smiled. "Perfect."

Katie laughed. "I aim to please."

His voice softened as he examined her face. "That you do."

His strong shoulders, wide chest and muscular stature filled her vision and seemed to dwarf the room. The bed at his back had never looked more welcoming.

"Time to go." After spinning toward the dresser, Katie grabbed her purse then headed for the door. "Don't want to be late, do we?"

A half hour later, they stood on packed Main Street in downtown Elk Valley where the spring festival was in full swing. A warm early-evening breeze swept over the small stretch of mountain road and the sweet smells of funnel cake, cotton candy and popcorn swirled around them. Boisterous talk and delighted laughter echoed off the small stores lining the road, and kids of all ages darted through groups of adults in all directions.

"Oh, no." Katie inched close to Landon's side and whispered, "I hope Heath's parents haven't let him near any sugar yet."

Landon glanced at her and raised an eyebrow. "Heath?"

"The little boy from practice last night." She lifted her hand. "Yay high? Throws food and is driving Melody closer to a breakdown with each school day?"

"Oh, yeah." He grinned. "Let's hope not."

Emma, standing five feet in front of them with Matthew at her side, jumped up and down and pointed at the crowd. "Look at the slides and the bounce house and the carousel. And all the people! Everyone in the whole world is here."

Katie cringed, a familiar nauseous sensation roiling in her belly. "It certainly feels that way."

Matthew looked over his shoulder. His face paled and his chin jerked on a hard swallow. "I can't do it."

Oh, boy. Neither could she.

Katie blew out a heavy breath and walked over on shaky legs, cupping his cheek in her palm. "Yes, you can."

"No." He shook his head. A strand of hair fell over his eyes. "I can't do the duet. I'll mess up and everyone will see."

A feeling she knew all too well. All her life, Katie had struggled with stage fright and Jennifer had been the only one who had ever managed to talk her out of running away from a stage in a screaming panic. Tonight was definitely not an exception. The only difference being that Jennifer wasn't here to bail her or Matthew out.

Digging deep, she tried to remember Jennifer's voice. Tried to recall the phrases Jennifer had used with her during pep talks over the years. But the distance between her and Jennifer now felt impossible to cross.

Katie forced herself to speak. "All they'll see is you doing a great job."

Matthew stared up at her, fear still prominent in his brown eyes. "I'll get it wrong. I won't be able to remember the words." His chin quivered. "I'll mess up the whole thing."

Stomach churning, Katie lowered to her knees and drew him close. "Then we'll mess up together, because I'm going to be with you the entire time. And we can handle anything so long as we're by each other's side." She firmed her voice. "Whatever happens, you won't be alone. I'll be right there with you."

He looked at the crowd milling around them then peered into her eyes, his expression hard. "You promise?"

She held his stare. "I promise."

Matthew watched her for a few moments then sniffed and seemed to collect himself. "Okay."

"Will you and Emma please round up the rest of the chorus members for me? Get everyone lined up by the stage like we practiced?"

He nodded. "We're gonna sing the group songs first, right? Then you and me will sing?"

"Yes. Just like we've done all week." She smiled. "It'll be great."

Satisfied with that, Matthew grabbed Emma's hand and they took off toward the stage.

Katie stood and someone waving from the edge of the crowd at the foot of the stage caught her eye.

"Katie," Patricia called out. "Send Landon over here. Your dad and I are right up front and we saved him the best seat in the house."

For her very public demise?

Katie's whole body shook and a cold chill froze every inch of her skin. She jumped as a boy chased another boy around her legs then into the crowd.

Landon's strong hand settled against the small of her back, its warm support steadying her as she spun to face him. A look of admiration filled his gaze.

"I…" Katie licked her lips and stared at that approving glint in his eyes, holding on to it. "I can do this, right? I just need someone to—"

"You can do this," Landon said firmly. "End of discussion."

Despite being on the verge of a meltdown, Katie managed a smile. "That's very matter-of-fact of you. Kinda bossy, even."

"So be it." Landon's mouth twitched. His eyes narrowed on her mouth as he nudged Sophia's stroller forward. "Now kiss Sophia and get your cute butt on that stage."

Normally, Landon didn't get nervous. There was no point. If something went wrong, he'd deal with it when it hit. And if things went well, being worried would have served no purpose.

But as Landon sat in front of the stage, trying to focus on Patricia's endless chatter while he waited for Katie to walk onto the stage with the kids, he had to admit tonight's circumstances had gotten the better of him.

"Are you listening to me?"

Shaking himself slightly, Landon focused on Patricia's concerned expression. "I'm sorry, what'd you say?"

"I said, I hope Katie is prepared. This concert is a tradition and it'd be a shame for it not to go well." Patricia waved Harold's words away as he moved to speak then asked, "And I've been meaning to ask, how is Katie doing with the kids lately? With Sophia, in particular?"

Landon studied Sophia as she sat in Patricia's arms, her mouth working around her pink pacifier, then looked at Harold. The other man sat silently by Patricia's side, a strained look on his face.

"Good," Landon answered. "Katie plays with her while I'm working, feeds her at mealtimes, bathes her." One corner of his mouth lifted. "Katie's even mastered the art of changing diapers."

Instead of the surprised but pleased expression he'd expected, Patricia looked down at Sophia, her brow creasing. "And how much longer is she staying?"

Landon's hand clenched around the program he held. "The kids are out of school next week for spring break. I'm assuming she'll stay until at least next Friday."

Or rather, he hoped she would. Katie hadn't mentioned it lately and he hadn't had the nerve to ask.

To be honest, he hadn't had much of a chance to dwell on it during the past week. Last Saturday, he'd been a bachelor, living alone in a quiet house on a ranch people rarely drove past on rural roads. But now, three children and a woman slept under his roof, greeted him every morning, ate breakfast beside him at his kitchen table then smiled up at him from their sprawled position on new furniture when he walked into the living room every evening.

But the moments he'd grown to look forward to the most were the handful of seconds between nine and ten at night. That brief window of time when Katie passed him on the way out of his bedroom, a quiet thank-you on her lips and a shy smile on her face, leaving a trail of aromatic mist behind her after soaking in his bathtub.

After she passed by him each night, Landon would stand in his bathroom, enveloped by the steam she'd left behind, staring at that bright bath bomb on his medicine shelf and wishing that instead of walking down the hall to slip into the guest bed, Katie would slip into his own.

And the kicker—the realization that had thumped inside his chest on more than one occasion over the past few days—was that he wished he could wake up to her every morning and experience the same wonderful day all over again on a permanent basis.

The kids' and Katie's presence had transformed his house. It had, just as Katie had said, become a home. And the five of them had begun to feel like a family to him. Not in the way Amber had feared, for the sake of convenience, but something different. Something more.

Landon stilled. He'd fallen in love with Katie. That attraction he'd always had to her had only strengthened since she returned to Elk Valley and this time, he knew he wanted to be more than friends. He wanted to marry her, and make a life with her here in Elk Valley.

If only Katie would consider giving up her life in

California to stay here and make a home with him. If only she felt the same way. Or maybe…she already did?

"And then?"

Landon blinked and met Patricia's eyes. "And then, what?"

"After spring break is over, will she leave?" Patricia urged, a flash of fear moving across her face. "Without the children?"

Without the…? A hollow feeling opened up in his gut. That was the kicker, wasn't it? If he told Katie he loved her and asked her to marry him, would she think he was only doing so as a convenient way of keeping the kids? Or, even worse, would she only accept the proposal out of a sense of obligation to Matthew, Emma and Sophia?

"She could still take them." Patricia's voice weakened as she cradled Sophia closer to her chest. "Katie told me last night she was interested in something more long-term with them, and you never know with Katie. As impulsive as she is, she may very well decide to load the kids up and haul them off with her. I just don't ever see her giving up her job in California to come back and live here. I know I may have given the impression that I'll only miss the kids, but I'll miss Katie terribly, too." She raised her gray head, tears in her eyes. "What would we do without all of them, Landon?"

Sophia, grinning behind her pacifier, babbled softly and reached out a hand toward Landon. He slipped his finger inside her tiny fist, a sad ache spreading through him as she squeezed.

"Good evening." Katie's voice hummed through the speakers on the stage.

He looked up, studying her face as she gripped the microphone and leaned in closer. She was nervous. It was right there in the small tremble of her voice and her white-knuckled grip on the mic.

"Elk Valley Elementary would like to welcome you to our annual spring concert." She smiled as the crowd applauded then waited for several couples to find seats and settle. "Our chorus will sing three selections as a whole group, then there'll be a short duet."

The mic squealed and, wincing, she stumbled back and gave a shaky smile.

"Oh, no." Landon reached for Sophia. "Come on, sweetheart. Let's give your aunt Katie a little encouragement."

Standing, he caught Katie's eye from the foot of the stage, waved Sophia's hand gently then winked. "You can do it, baby," he whispered.

Katie's smile steadied, and she returned to the mic. "We hope you enjoy."

Landon waited as she took her seat at the piano. Feeling Patricia's eyes on him, he returned Sophia to her lap and managed a smile.

So many emotions flickered through her expression. Surprised confusion. Pride tinged with a bit of sadness. Fear. And it was the fear on her face that stayed with him as the kids filed onto the stage, filled the choral risers and began to sing in time with Katie's playing and Melody's lead.

The group sang as well as they had last night. Several boys wore frog hats and a lot of the girls had bumblebee stripes or butterfly wings, and they belted out tunes celebrating flowers, wildlife and the joys of springtime in general. Their voices rose as one and, despite a missed note or ill-placed verse or two, the kids performed as fantastically as Landon had hoped.

It wasn't long before Melody's arms slowed and the final group song drew to a close. The rows and rows of cell phones recording in midair lowered and parents clapped, laughing and spreading their arms wide as their sons and daughters skipped off stage and sat with the audience.

Throughout the performance, the sky surrounding Main Street had darkened and night had fallen. The moon, full and bright, rose high, silhouetting the mountain range behind the raised stage and spilling a pool of white light across the piano where Katie and Matthew sat side by side on a bench.

The crowd grew quiet. Katie shared a look with Matthew, whispered something then moved her hands over the keys. Gentle chords rose from the black piano, lifting into the starlit night and floating over the crowd.

Moments later, Katie's melodic voice emerged. Her slow verses swept over the crowd, silencing nearby chatter on the sidewalks, calming bystanders' movements at vendors' stands, and evoking a collective stillness throughout Main Street.

Matthew's voice joined her during the chorus then took over the next lyrics. His words shook at first then gradually steadied, drawing strength from Katie's soothing tone. The more Katie played and the more they sang, the closer they leaned into each other on the bench.

Soon, Katie eased back on the bench, her voice receding, and Matthew's grew stronger. His chin lifted, his chest billowed with each of his breaths and he belted out each note perfectly.

A soft sound escaped Harold. He squeezed Patricia's hand at Sophia's back then glanced at Landon with tears on his lashes.

"That's a little bit of our baby right there," Harold said, gesturing toward Matthew. "My Jennifer's still living through our beautiful grandson." He looked at Patricia, determination in his eyes. "Our sweet Katie did that. I don't ever want to hear you say she doesn't love those kids again."

Patricia nodded. Pride, joy and sorrow flitted over her expression as she stared down at their entwined hands cradling Sophia.

When the final note faded, Harold shot to his feet, clapped his hands and shouted, "Those are my babies right there!" His smile grew as the crowd around them laughed and cheered. He pumped his fist in the air. "Good job, babies!"

Throat tight, Landon stood with him and clapped. The same pride that lifted Harold's chest spread throughout his own.

Katie and Matthew rose, rounded the bench and, after taking each other's hand, bowed. The applause grew louder. A big smile broke out across Matthew's face and he turned to the side and hugged Katie, wrapping his arms tight around her and rocking her back on her heels.

Katie regained her balance and hugged him back. Laughing, she met Landon's eyes then mouthed, *"Thank you."*

Landon nodded then watched as Katie and Matthew walked off the stage. The sight of their retreating backs as they moved farther and farther away pierced his heart a little deeper.

Chapter 9

Funnel cake, cotton candy and popcorn consumed on a sidewalk during a spring festival did not constitute a healthy, well-balanced family meal. But boy, did it taste like heaven.

"Want some more cotton candy, Aunt Katie?" Emma stifled a yawn then held out a white stick topped with a small pink cloud of sugar.

Katie groaned and rubbed her overstuffed stomach. "Oh, no. I think I've had enough."

"Aw, come on." Landon, standing nearby, plucked a chunk of cotton candy from the stick and held it up. "You're not gonna let one handful of cotton candy force you to wimp out on a night of fun?"

Katie raised an eyebrow. "Now, wait just a minute. Did I not play in the bounce house with Emma—in a dress, mind you—throw darts with Matthew, hold my own on the inflatable slides with you and get my face painted?" She tapped the colorful butterfly on her cheek. "I think I've earned my fun stripes tonight."

Landon eyed her cheek and grinned. "Nope. That particular face paint doesn't count."

"Why not?"

"Not tough enough." He shared a smile with Matthew. "If it were a skull and crossbones—" he shrugged "—maybe. But a butterfly..."

"No dice," Matthew said, laughing.

Landon chuckled. It was soft and short-lived but a laugh just the same.

Katie smiled. It was so wonderful to hear Landon laugh again. Two hours ago, after the chorus concert, Landon and Emma had met Katie and Matthew backstage and they'd wandered off to explore the festival activities while her mom and dad watched Sophia. It was a beautiful night and the later it became, the more the crowd had thinned out, leaving short lines, minimal waiting and tons of fun to be had.

Only, Landon had remained relatively quiet at first and hadn't loosened up until after his and Emma's second cherry slush and three trips down the inflatable slide.

Oh, the slide. Katie smiled. That had been her favorite. Speeding down an eighteen-foot slide with Landon's arms and legs wrapped around her from behind, the wind whipping through her hair and his muscular chest rumbling with laughter against her back. She couldn't remember a single date in her past that had made her stomach turn somersaults like exploring the festival with Landon had.

Wait. A date? This wasn't a date. This was—

"If you want to earn your official fun stripes, you'll eat one more bite." Landon lifted the cotton candy to her lips. "It's barely enough to fill a tablespoon."

Katie grinned. "All right. One more bite and that's it for me."

She opened her mouth and Landon placed it on her tongue, the blunt tips of his fingers brushing her lower lip as he removed his hand. She closed her mouth and the sweet concoction melted, her face heating as Landon brought his fingers to his own mouth to suck off the residual sugar.

Landon's eyes met hers, the blue depths darkening, and his lean cheeks flushed.

"Having fun?"

They both jumped at the sound of her mother's voice. Katie coughed as the dissolved sugar trickled down her throat and Landon wiped his hand on his jeans and looked away.

Patricia walked up, Sophia sleeping in her arms and Harold pushing the stroller.

"Am I interrupting something?" Patricia asked, glancing between the two of them, a hopeful gleam in her eyes.

"Not at all." Landon found his voice first. "We were just thinking of calling it a night."

That blank look fell over his face, masking his expression. Katie licked the last taste of sugar from her lips then whispered, "A fun night."

A half smile crossed his magnificent lips. "Yeah."

"Which is why," Patricia continued, beckoning Emma

over with a wave of her hand, "Harold and I thought we'd offer to let the kids stay with us tonight."

Katie stared at her mother, noting the way she kept avoiding direct eye contact. "Wait, why?"

"Why?" Patricia's shoulder lifted near her ears and an innocent expression crossed her face. "Do I need a reason to invite my grandchildren over for a visit?"

Landon frowned. "It's late, Patricia. The kids are exhausted."

"As are the two of you," Harold said, holding out his hand to Matthew. "Our place is only five minutes up the road and yours is almost a half hour away. If the kids jump in the car and go home with us, they'll get a good night's sleep and have an early-morning breakfast with Gammie and Papa. And you and Katie can go back to the ranch, catch your breath for one night then rise at your leisure."

Katie narrowed her eyes and mulled it over. She had to admit, the arrangement did make sense and being able to sleep in on a Sunday was something she never turned up her nose at. "I suppose. That is, if it's okay with Landon?"

He looked at Sophia peacefully sleeping for a few moments then said, "All right. What do you think, kids?"

Matthew tugged Katie's hand. "Will you pick us up tomorrow, Aunt Katie?"

Katie nodded. "Of course."

Matthew turned back to Harold. "Then that's cool."

Half an hour later, Katie and Landon returned to the ranch and Rascal greeted them at the door.

"Hey, buddy." Landon scratched Rascal behind his

ears and rubbed his neck then tossed his keys on the hall table.

They stood there for a few moments, staring at each other. Other than Rascal's soft panting, it was a lot quieter than when the kids were around. Way too quiet. Strangely quiet, almost.

"I'm gonna check on the horses," Landon blurted. He headed for the door then hesitated. "You...uh, want to use my tub again tonight?"

Katie shifted from one foot to the other then picked a popcorn hull off the hem of her skirt and thumped it toward the floor. "Yes. I need a good bath." She gave an awkward laugh. "Think I carried home half the festival with me."

"Have at it. I'll shower after you finish." He dragged a hand across the back of his neck. "Well, I'll leave you to it."

Landon left, and Rascal scampered after him.

Katie sighed, slid off her shoes then made her way to the guest bedroom. She parted the curtains and looked out the window. With the absence of streetlights, the moon was brighter at Landon's ranch. It bathed the fields in a white glow and outlined Landon's muscular figure as he strode to the stable.

She crossed her arms and hugged her chest, a small smile lifting her mouth as she remembered the feel of his strong arms around her on the slide. The stubble on his jaw grazing the sensitive skin below her ear and his husky chuckle tickling her neck. Those excited flutters in her belly at his touch, his warm nearness.

Everything about the moment had felt new and exciting and the whole night had been a delight. So much so, it left her feeling like a kid again.

A laugh escaped her and she spun away from the window, her skirt twirling around her bare legs as she danced over to the dresser. Her bag caught her eye and she dug around in it until she found a yellow bath bomb. She lifted it to her nose, closed her eyes and inhaled, the scent reminiscent of warm sunshine, fresh air and open fields a kid could roll in for days.

"That's it." Smiling, she fished a piece of paper and pen out of her bag then carried all three items to Landon's bathroom.

She set the bath bomb on Landon's medicine shelf beside the beige one, wrote on the paper then propped it against the yellow sphere.

Be a Kid.

That was exactly how she'd felt tonight, singing the duet with Matthew, eating cotton candy with Emma and holding Sophia on the carousel. She couldn't wait to show the three of them around California. First, she'd take them to the beach, help them find seashells and wade in the ocean. Then she'd take them to the museum, aquarium and libr—

But wait. That would mean taking them away from Landon. A man who loved them. A man she...

"Katie, you decent?"

She stilled, her hand on the medicine shelf. "Yeah."

Landon peeked around the open door of the bathroom then, after scanning her appearance, walked into the room. He motioned toward the medicine shelf. "Come up with a new name?"

Katie nodded. "Yep. It has an invigorating scent that

lifts the spirit and leaves you feeling giddy. It suits tonight's fun, I think, don't you?"

He smiled. "You and Matthew sounded great. The entire chorus did, too. He and Emma were so happy tonight. You've worked wonders with them."

"Because of you. Again." She grinned. "Thank you for the pep talk."

"You're welcome." He shoved his hands in his pockets, glanced around then looked at her from under his lashes. "Tonight, your mom asked me how much longer you were staying."

"She did?" Katie held her breath as he nodded. "What'd you tell her?"

"What should I have told her?"

That was the ten-million-dollar question. She bit her lip. How could she say that she'd probably pack hers and the kids' things midweek then fly them all to California and get them settled? How could she tell Landon that she was taking the kids from him? Or…could she consider leaving them for his sake?

No. That part, she finally conceded to herself, wasn't up for debate. She couldn't possibly leave without Matthew, Emma and Sophia. No matter how much it would hurt Landon.

The thought made her catch her breath, her vision blurring.

Unable to face him, Katie dropped her hand to her side. "I don't know. I was thinking about heading back on Monday. I'm scheduled to do a presentation on Friday and that'd give me time to prepare without having to rush."

Landon crossed the room slowly, stopping close in

front of her. So close, the warmth of his body drifted around her. "It'll take some getting used to."

"What will?"

"Not having you around."

Surprise rippled through her. Katie blinked hard then looked up, her eyes meeting his. "M-me?"

"Yeah." His hand lifted, hesitated and then drifted through the ends of her hair. "I'll miss that cute bounce of yours."

Her brows rose. "My bounce?"

He smiled. "The one you do when you're thanking me." His gaze fell to her mouth, his eyes heating. "Right before you kiss me."

Her breath escaped her on a shaky sigh. "Oh."

"As a matter of fact," he said, leaning closer, "I miss it already. I've been missing it for days now." He touched his palms to the wall, one on either side of her. "I'd really like to kiss you again. Hold you. Maybe more if you wanted me, too."

"I…" Her voice failed her, her senses absorbing the sensation of his nearness. His sexily rumpled hair, strong jaw and sculpted mouth. The desire in his eyes and slight quickening of his breath. "I'd like that."

The moment the words left her mouth, his lips parted hers. His tongue swept past her teeth, his masculine taste making her legs weak and body hum. He slid a muscular thigh between her knees, her silk skirt catching on a crease in his jeans and stretching tight against her skin.

His broad hand left the wall and slid down her side, massaging as it moved, cupping her breast, her hip, her thighs, then it slipped beneath her skirt and lifted the hem. He eased his hard hips tighter between her thighs.

A moan left her mouth and entered his, their breaths mingling as he cradled her snugly against him. She'd never felt so safe, protected and cherished.

And she owed him the truth now. At least so he'd have time to give the children a proper goodbye.

"Landon…"

She pulled back and tried to speak. Tried to tell him how much she didn't want to hurt him. That the only reason she'd decided to fulfil Jennifer's wishes was because she loved Matthew, Emma and Sophia too much to leave them behind. That she loved the kids as much as she loved him.

Her breath caught in her throat, the realization momentarily stunning her. Somewhere along the way, she'd fallen in *love* with Landon. And it would break her heart to leave and take the children from him.

"Is something wrong?" His hands stilled as he stared down at her, concern warring with the fierce need in his eyes.

Katie couldn't tell him. Not now. Not when he held her in his arms.

"No," she whispered, touching her mouth to his. "Just love me."

Katie's words were all the encouragement Landon needed.

Bending, he slipped his arms beneath her knees, then lifted her in his arms and carried her into his bedroom. He lowered her gently to the bed then stood motionless for a moment, admiring the spill of her dark hair across the pillow, the rise and fall of her soft breasts beneath the green silk of her dress and the sprawling length of her toned limbs across his white sheets.

The sight of her in his bed was more perfect than he'd imagined and stirred a longing deep within him for something more. Something real and lasting. A committed partnership for life.

He hadn't wanted that before. But he wanted it more than anything now.

She opened her arms and he lowered into them, nudging her thighs apart, settling his chest against hers and nuzzling her neck. Her hands roamed over his shoulders and back then slipped beneath the waistband of his jeans and tugged.

Gradually, they removed each other's clothes and the exquisite glide of her silky breasts against his hair-roughened chest made him groan. He trailed kisses everywhere. Over the curves of her breasts, across her belly then lower, her breathless gasp and the arch of her hips urging him on.

And when he donned protection and joined his body to hers, he buried his face in the fall of her hair, breathed her in and hung on, only giving in himself when he felt her tighten around him, heard her cry of pleasure and felt her tremble in his arms.

Afterward, he rolled to his back and took her with him, lifting her leg over his hip and tucking her head beneath his chin.

Her lips brushed his chest and her rapid breaths rippled over his skin as she struggled to speak. "That was…"

Landon smiled.

"Wonderful," Katie finished, nuzzling tighter against him.

"Yeah."

It had been. Still was, even. He could feel her heartbeat, strong and excited, pounding against his own. The scent of fresh mountain air clung to her hair and the sweet flavor of cotton candy—from her mouth and his own—lingered on every inch of their skin.

They'd carried a little piece of a fantastic night home, shared their excitement with each other and held it between them now, savoring it.

Katie's laughter tickled his chest.

Landon glanced down to find her grinning up at him. "What?"

"You've earned your fun stripe, too." She ran her fingertip over a tiny spot of multicolored paint on his abs. "You're sporting half my butterfly now."

He chuckled then kissed what was left of the face paint on her cheek. "Real fun is messy, I guess."

Her smile faded and a look of dismay crossed her expression. "Oh, no." She squeezed her eyes shut then planted her face against his chest, mumbling, "I've just given credence to Elk Valley rumors and done exactly what my mother has been telling people I haven't."

"What rumors?"

"That I'm living with you—" she lifted her head, her brown eyes blinking up at him "—in a carnal sense."

His mouth twitched, and he hugged her closer, thinking of how much like heaven it would be to have Katie living with him—and not just in a carnal sense, but as his wife.

"Would that be so bad?" He stilled as the words left his lips. "You living here in Elk Valley again?"

Katie remained silent for a moment as she studied him then whispered, "I don't know." Her palm moved in slow circles on his skin, right over his heart. "I've spent years building a life in California. My friends and my career are there. A promotion I've spent a long time earning with responsibilities I can't ignore."

Landon tried to hide the disappointment washing over him. "Like your presentation on Friday?"

"Yes."

He pulled in a deep breath. "Would you consider staying with me and the kids until Tuesday? Matthew and Emma are out of school next week and we could take them camping Monday night. We could have one more night of fun before you leave."

And he might have one more shot at talking her into staying. Of persuading her to consider making a new life here with the kids…and with him.

"Okay," she whispered. "Then Tuesday, it'll be time to leave."

Katie moved to say more, pain flashing in her eyes, but lowered her cheek against his chest instead.

Fears returning, he smoothed a hand over her hair. "What is it, Katie?"

She shook her head, her voice hesitant. "Nothing. I'm just thinking about my presentation. I still have one bath bomb left in the collection to name."

He smiled. "What color is it?"

"Pink." She laughed softly. "Like cotton candy, with lots of bubbles that smell just as sweet. There are so many they rise up to your chin if you're not careful and almost overflow the tub. When I used them last night, they almost spilled over. I thought I'd ruin your bathroom tile. Those bubbles aren't like any of the others."

He thought of the other name she'd created—*Be a Kid*—and how she'd said it suited tonight's fun. "How do they feel when you're in them?"

A sound of contentment escaped her. "Sexy and comforting. Exciting, peaceful and a little scary, all at once."

Landon hugged her closer and touched his lips to her hair, his heart aching. "Like being in love."

Chapter 10

Landon loaded the last sleeping bag in the bed of his truck, double-checked that all four backpacks were safely tied down then handed Nate the keys to his house.

"I really appreciate your taking care of things around here, man. And for babysitting Sophia." He looked over Nate's shoulder and waved. Sophia smiled at him from Amber's arms as she stood on the other side of the driveway waiting for Nate. "You have no idea how important this night is to me."

Nate shrugged. "Not a problem, but camping should be fun. You've sounded nothing but stressed since you called me this morning. What makes this trip up the mountain so different than all the others?"

Landon watched as Katie, Matthew and Emma emerged from his house, each of them laughing and carrying a fishing pole and a few bags of snacks. "Katie is leaving tomorrow afternoon." Throat tightening, he swallowed hard. "And I think she's going to tell me she's taking the kids with her."

Nate frowned and glanced over his shoulder as Katie and the kids stopped to speak to Amber. "You don't think you've been able to convince her that they're better off here with you?"

Landon looked down and scraped the toe of his boot across the dirt. "That's the thing. Katie's worked hard at being a good aunt. I mean, you and Amber saw for yourselves how well she did with the school chorus at the festival. She's comfortable watching Sophia now and she's earned Matthew's and Emma's trust." He dragged a hand over his face. "She loves them, and there's not a single reason why the kids wouldn't be in good hands with her."

"But?"

"I don't want to let them go." He reached inside his jeans pocket, pulled out a small velvet box and flipped open the lid. "Not even Katie."

Nate whistled low as he stared at the diamond ring. "One week, man?" His brows rose. "She roped you in in one week?"

Landon shook his head. "Longer than that. I've always admired her from afar over the years, but having her here…" The corners of his mouth lifted as he thought over the past few days. "She loves the kids so much. She's dedicated to them. She's funny and sweet— not to mention beautiful and sexy. She makes me laugh. Makes me feel like I'm alive. Makes my house feel like a home." He laughed. "She leaves her bras hanging in my bathroom. Soaks in my tub with bubbles that smell so damned delicious, and the sweet scent lingers in my bedroom for hours and drives me insane." His chest warmed. "She's damn near everywhere. In my head, in my heart."

Nate smiled in Amber's direction. "I know the feeling." He faced Landon again. "But didn't I tell you not to let her in your bathroom?"

Landon laughed. "You did."

"That's right." Nate jabbed his finger against Landon's chest. "Don't ever say I never gave you good advice or wasn't a good friend to you."

"Nah." Landon closed the velvet box and slipped it back inside his pocket. "You're a great friend. Just cross your fingers that my proposal goes over well tonight and that Katie decides to stay."

"A great guy like you proposing?" Nate gave a crooked grin. "There's no way she'll turn you down."

An hour later, driving his truck up a steep mountain road, Landon hoped Nate was right.

"Can we go swimming in the river?" Emma piped up from the back seat of the cab.

Landon looked at her in the rearview mirror and smiled. "Sure. We can show Katie your favorite spot."

"And can we take Aunt Katie fishing?" Matthew asked from beside Emma.

"If she wants." Landon glanced at Katie, who sat in the passenger seat. "Whatcha say, Katie?"

"Hmm?" Katie turned away from the window and faced him, a distracted look in her eyes. "I'm sorry, what?"

Landon smiled. "Matthew asked if we could take you fishing. Is that something you'd like to do?"

Katie released a heavy breath and gave a small smile. "Sure. I'd like that."

There were shadows under her eyes. Ones that had shown up Sunday morning after the night they'd made love, and they were still there earlier this morning when he'd left to drive into town and buy the engagement ring. He'd tried to get her to open up and tell him what was worrying her twice, but each time she'd waved away his concern, excused herself to return to her work then glued her attention to her laptop instead.

He knew what was bothering her. It showed in her eyes, strained expression and half-hearted smile. Katie had decided to fulfil Jennifer's wishes, assume her role as primary guardian and take the kids with her to California. And she couldn't bring herself to tell him.

"It's okay," Landon said softly. At Katie's look of confusion, he waited until he cleared the top of the mountain then removed one hand from the steering wheel, covering hers in her lap. "Don't worry about work or anything else right now. We're going to have a great night of camping. It'll be as much fun as the festival."

Or at least, he hoped it would. It had to be. Because he was beginning to believe what Nate had said. That there was no way Katie would turn his offer of marriage down because she loved him as much as he loved her. He'd felt it in her tender touch right there in his bed, and when she looked up at him as he moved over her, he'd seen it reflected in her eyes. He was sure of it.

"Do you ever go fishing in Los Angeles, Aunt Katie?"

Landon's hand froze around Katie's as Matthew leaned closer to the back of her seat, waiting for her answer.

Katie cleared her throat. "Not much. But there's a place called Diamond Valley Lake about an hour and a half away from my apartment. I have a friend who goes there a lot for black bass. She's caught bluegill and trout there, too."

Matthew smiled. "Cool."

"What about swimming?" Emma asked. "Do you ever go swimming?"

Katie perked up. "Oh, all the time. The beach is only a few blocks from my place. It's warm almost all the time and there's nothing better for stress than playing in the waves."

Matthew leaned closer. "Are they big?"

Katie laughed. "Huge, sometimes." She twisted in her seat to face him. "And I have a surfboard. I'm not very good at surfing but I give it my best shot."

"Could we try it sometime?" Emma asked, bouncing in her seat.

"Of course you can." Katie waved her hands with excitement. "And there's an art museum and aquarium I'd love to take you to. And—"

Katie stopped talking, glanced under her lashes in Landon's direction then turned back in her seat to face the road.

It fell silent in the cab, save for the noise of the engine and the squeak of brakes as Landon parked the truck. He withdrew the keys from the ignition, pressed them against the ring bulging in his pocket then looked at Katie. Her cheeks were red and her lips trembled.

The kids sat motionless in the back seat, staring down at their hands, their smiles disappearing.

"Matthew?" Landon waited until he met his eyes

in the rearview mirror. "Feel like walking with me to round up some firewood for roasting marshmallows tonight?"

Matthew looked up, a small smile appearing. "Yes, sir."

Thank God. Landon needed to stretch his legs, breathe fresh air and talk himself into believing things were going to work out fine. That this new life with Katie and the kids was truly a possibility and that despite the attractive alternatives, Katie would say yes to marrying him and choose to stay. Not just for the kids, but because she loved him.

Tonight, by the campfire, he'd propose. Katie would say yes, and they'd finally be a true family.

Landon smiled back at Matthew "All right, let's hit it. We're burning daylight."

Twenty minutes later, Landon and Matthew finished setting up two tents then walked down a winding dirt path to hunt for firewood. Katie stayed behind with Emma to unroll the sleeping bags and explore the campsite.

"Look for large branches that may have fallen," Landon said, leading the way through the woods.

Matthew stopped beside a dead-looking branch that was propped against a canopy of leaves. He grabbed a small, protruding limb, snapped a portion off and handed it to Landon. "What about this? Is it dry enough?"

Landon nodded. "Perfect. Now, let's find about twenty more like that."

For the next few minutes, the only sounds in the surrounding woods were birds, the swish of thick leaves and snaps of twigs underfoot. Landon lifted an armload of wood he'd found and noticed Matthew's arms were loaded down, too.

"Good job, buddy. Follow me." Landon swept a low-hanging branch out of the way, ducked and led Matthew into a small clearing. "Dump what you've got here and let's take a break before heading back." He pointed toward the edge of an overlook several feet away. "There's a great view over there."

They walked over, staying a safe distance from the edge, and took in the view below. Tall trees and green growth dotted the towering tops of mountain ranges in the distance and a swift breeze blew with a slight whistle across the drop below. There wasn't a cloud in sight and the blue sky seemed to stretch endlessly to the rocky horizon.

"Gorgeous." Landon inhaled, holding the fresh air in his lungs. "Your aunt Amber and I used to come up here when we were kids. It felt like it took forever to make it up the trail and get to this spot but it was always our favorite." He lifted his face and closed his eyes, enjoying the warmth of the sun seeping past his closed eyelids. "There's a creek a bit farther down with these odd-shaped rocks that me and Amber used to build forts. It's beautiful and I think Emma and Katie would like it." Patting the ring in his pocket absently, he turned to the side and smiled down at Matthew. "We could—"

Matthew's shoulders jerked and a choked sob burst from his lips.

"Hey." Landon swept his hand through Matthew's hair then cupped his cheek, lifting his chin for a better view of his face. A big tear pooled in the corner of Matthew's trembling mouth. "What's this about?"

"I…I can't—" Matthew looked away, his breath snagging.

Landon waited for a moment, concerned confusion streaking through him, and when Matthew didn't speak, he said, "You can tell me anything, you know that. What's going on?"

Matthew studied the ground, whispering something unintelligible.

Landon leaned closer. "What?"

Matthew lifted his head, his brown eyes pained. "I don't want to hurt you."

"You don't want to…?" Landon shook his head, a confused smile lifting his mouth. "How could you hurt me?"

"I don't want to live with you anymore."

The words hit Landon's chest like rocks, each one cracking his heart a bit more. "Wh-what? What are you talking ab—"

"I mean, I do want to live with you," Matthew said through sobs. "But I want to live with Aunt Katie more." He sucked in a deep breath, the tears coming fast now. "Me and Emma both do. I heard Aunt Katie tell Gammie on the phone that she's going back to California tomorrow and we wanna go with her."

Legs weak, Landon sank to his knees in front of Matthew and squeezed his shoulders. "You…" His voice sounded choked. He cleared his throat. "Have you talked to Katie about this?"

Matthew shook his head, his hair falling over his eyes. "No. I w-wanted to tell you first."

Landon couldn't speak. Couldn't move. Could barely breathe.

All he could do was listen to Matthew's words repeating in his mind and stabbing him on the inside. *I don't want to live with you.*

Oh, God. Landon turned his head and closed his eyes. That wasn't what he had said. Not really. He had said he wanted to live with Katie, and of course he would. He'd want to fish in Diamond Valley Lake, swim in the ocean waves and visit all of the exciting attractions near Katie's apartment in Los Angeles. He wanted to live in a vibrant, bustling city a thousand times bigger and more exciting than a small ranch in Elk Valley.

And every step he'd helped Katie take toward being a good parent had coaxed the kids further and further away from him. How could he not have seen it? And if he had, would he have still helped her?

"Uncle Landon?"

He opened his eyes and Matthew's pained expression made his stomach churn. Matthew had been afraid to tell him, and now, after he had, he felt guilty for having hurt him.

"I'm sorry, Uncle Landon. I'm so sor—"

"No." Landon tugged him forward and hugged him hard, wanting to scream, to cry, to rage at the unfairness of it all. But what he wanted more was for Matthew, Emma, Sophia and Katie to be happy. "You have nothing to be sorry for." He kissed Matthew's cheek, ruffled his hair and strived for an upbeat tone. "It's okay. I understand."

Fresh tears brimmed in Matthew's eyes. "But…"

"I love you," Landon said firmly, cupping his face

and meeting his eyes. "Always. I want you to be happy."
He forced a smile. "So no more crying, okay? This is a
good thing, and I know your aunt Katie will be thrilled."

Matthew blinked up at him, searching his eyes, then
wiped his face on his sleeve. "Okay."

Landon pushed slowly to his feet, his body heavy
and hurting. "Why don't you take a load of the firewood
back to camp and help Katie build a fire?"

Matthew nodded, gathered up an armful of firewood
then paused at the edge of the clearing. "Aren't you
coming?"

Landon turned away, hiding the wet heat streaming down his cheeks. "Yeah. I'll be right behind you."

Twigs snapped and leaves rustled as Matthew left
then Landon stood alone, staring at the view beyond, his
chest tight with silent sobs. There was no way he could
tell Katie he loved her, ask her to marry him and live in
Elk Valley now. Not when he knew Matthew and Emma
wanted to go to California with Katie, and not when there
was a chance of Katie thinking he only wanted to marry
her as a way of holding on to the kids. And it would be
selfish to ask her to give up her job and life in Los Angeles solely for him.

Katie was related to Matthew, Emma and Sophia by
blood; Landon was just a family friend. He had no right
to interfere.

Landon shoved the ring deeper into his pocket and
clenched his fists as he studied the peaceful sky above
him. It was a hell of a thing. The birds sang and the sun
shone bright despite the fact that every hope he'd had
for a life with Katie and the kids in Elk Valley had just

died. It was the first time, Landon realized, that helping someone else find happiness had cost him his own.

"Can I have one more?"

Katie glanced across the campfire at Emma as she scooted closer to Landon's side and held out her stick. The bright blaze of the fire pierced their dark surroundings and lit up her excited expression.

"I suppose that's okay." Landon reached into the bag at his side and grabbed a marshmallow.

Katie watched the play of firelight across the muscles in his strong forearm as he affixed the treat to the stick then helped Emma hold it over the heat. His blue eyes remained focused on the flames, unblinking at the crackle of wood and occasional spit of sparks. His demeanor, silent and downcast, had remained unchanged since he'd returned from collecting firewood with Matthew several hours ago.

"Matthew?" Katie waited until he lifted his head and faced her from his seated position on a log. "Would you like another marshmallow?"

Matthew shook his head then stood. "I'm kinda tired. Think I'll go to bed now." He walked over to Landon, hesitating slightly before leaning down to hug him. "Good night, Uncle Landon."

Landon, a smile crossing his face, returned the hug, but the smile vanished as he watched Matthew walk away then enter one of the tents.

"Blow it out, blow it out," Emma squealed, tugging at her flaming marshmallow.

Landon quickly put the flame out, pinched it to test

the heat level then passed it to Emma. "Be careful. Don't burn your mouth."

Emma did a little dance as she ate it then licked her fingers and rubbed her belly. "That was good. Can I have another one?"

"'Fraid not, baby." Landon's voice was strangely heavy. "It's time for bed."

Emma made a sound of disappointment but hugged Landon and skipped around the fire to Katie. "Night, Aunt Katie."

"Good night, angel." Katie kissed her cheek then smiled as she crawled inside a tent. "This trip was a great idea," she said, looking at Landon. "I'm glad we came."

Landon seemed to try to smile but it fell flat, and he patted the empty space on the log beside him. "We need to talk, Katie."

And there it was. The moment Katie had been dreading. She could see the dismay on his face, heard it in his voice. He already knew what she hadn't had the guts to tell him.

Sighing, Katie stood, brushed off the back of her jeans then rounded the fire and sat beside him. The log was warm beneath her and she curled her palm around it by her side, her pinky touching Landon's as he did the same.

"Are you still planning to leave tomorrow?" His deep voice sounded raspy in the dim glow of the fire.

Katie nodded. "There's a flight around four that I'd like to catch. That'd give me at least a little extra time before my presentation Friday afternoon."

Oh, boy. No more putting it off. But how should

she say it? Which words should she use? What phrase would hurt him less?

She pulled in a shaky breath. "Landon, I'm planning to—"

"Matthew wants to go with you."

She stilled. "What?"

"Emma, too." Only Landon's mouth moved as he stared at the fire. "He told me himself this afternoon."

His voice sounded strange and heavy and his jaw tightened. He was hurting. So much more than she'd imagined.

Her stomach dropped. "Oh, Landon."

Katie swiveled toward him, cradled his face and rubbed her thumbs over his cheeks. The stubble lining his jaw was rough against her fingertips and the slight tremor in his chin almost undid her.

"I didn't want us to be put in this position with the kids," she whispered. "I never suggested it or asked for it. I don't know why Jennifer asked it of me, and I never in a million years would want to do anything that would hurt you."

"I know." His hands circled her wrists and he kissed her face, touching his mouth to her fluttering lashes, drifting his lips across her cheeks. "I know," he repeated, his husky whisper near her ear. "But you were going to do what Jennifer asked, weren't you? You were already planning to take Matthew, Emma and Sophia?"

Katie froze, pain flooding her. "Yes. I planned to take all three of them with me to California."

"And you love them?"

She stifled a sob. "Of course, I do. More than anything."

"Then that's all that matters." He pulled away and made to stand.

"Landon." She grabbed his arm and helplessly studied the angry pain in his eyes, unsure of what to say.

"We'll head back to the ranch first thing in the morning and pack their things." He stood anyway. "Some of it I'll have to send to you later. And I assume you want them to visit with Harold and Patricia before they leave?"

"Landon, please." Katie jumped to her feet and placed her hands on his chest, blinking back tears. "Don't be angry with me. Please don't hate me over this."

His expression gentled. "Never."

He wrapped his arms around her, pulled her close and covered her mouth with his. His kiss was warm and gentle, and when the salty taste of tears hit their tongues, he released her.

"You'll visit us, won't you?" Katie asked, her arms feeling empty without him to hold on to. "Even if it's just for a day or two? The kids will miss you terribly and you might like LA."

Landon stayed silent for a moment then said, "Maybe one day." He turned away, saying over his shoulder, "We'll pack up and head back to the ranch around seven."

Katie watched him walk away and enter the same tent as Matthew. It grew silent and still, save for the pop and crackle of the fire. She stayed there for another two hours, watching the fire, replaying the events of the past week and missing Jennifer more than ever. This fantastic new start with the kids should feel wonderful but taking them away from Landon made her feel awful.

* * *

The next day was no better.

"Can I take Jinx?"

Katie closed the packed box in front of her, taped it shut then shook her head at Matthew, who sat on his bed as they packed the last of his belongings. "I'm sorry, but we can't. Not on a plane."

Besides, she was already trying to figure out how to juggle Sophia's stroller and all of their bags to and from the airport.

"Don't worry about Jinx," Landon said, picking up the box. "I'll take good care of him."

"But when will we see him again?" Emma asked from the doorway, clutching a blue teddy bear. "Are we coming back in a few days?"

Katie moved to answer then stopped, biting her lip as Landon ducked his head and left the room. "We'll visit, baby," she said softly. "As soon as we can."

Emma turned, looking down the hall in the direction Landon had gone. "But when?"

"In a couple weeks, maybe. After we get settled." Katie closed her eyes for a moment, holding back more tears she refused to shed in front of the kids. "Then in a few months, it'll be Thanksgiving. That might be a good time to come back again."

"I expect it to be a good time." Patricia walked into the room, holding Sophia, then leveled a look at Katie. "Because I'll miss all of you very much and I plan on cooking enough to feed an army." Her mouth trembled then she lifted her chin and smiled. "I hope it'll be okay if I visit from time to time."

Katie blinked hard. "You…you want to come visit me in California?"

Patricia nodded then gave a self-conscious laugh. "Guess I finally figured out that planes are capable of traveling in both directions. I'd love to see your apartment and the kids. I'd love to see you, Katie."

"In that case," Katie said, "I'd be really happy if you could come see us next weekend? Bring some of the kids' things they had to leave behind and help us settle in?"

Patricia smiled, her eyes wet. "That would be wonderful."

An hour later, Katie stuffed the bags in the trunk of the rental car, hugged and kissed her parents then watched as they drove away. She checked that Sophia was strapped safely in her car seat then shut the door.

"Well—" Katie clapped her hands together and faced Landon "—I guess it's time we head out."

"Uncle Landon?" Emma ran over and tugged at Landon's shirt. "Will you call us tonight?"

Landon squatted and kissed Emma's cheek. "If it's okay with your aunt Katie?"

"Yes." Katie stilled her weight on the tips of her toes, resisting the urge to walk into his embrace, too. "Call us anytime. Every day, if you'd like."

Katie hoped he would. Way more than she had any right to expect.

"Bye, Uncle Landon." Matthew ran over and hugged Landon tight, the quiet sound of his sobs bringing tears to Katie's eyes.

After saying goodbye, Matthew and Emma hopped in the car and buckled up then looked expectantly out the window at Katie.

Turning her back to the car, she walked over to Landon and threw her arms around him. She buried her face in his neck and held on, wondering how she'd ever manage to let go.

His hands were in her hair, winding the strands loosely around his fingers, then he dipped his head, his lips moving against her cheek. "You're gonna miss your flight."

She squeezed her eyes shut. "Landon?"

"Yeah?" His palms drifted over her back.

"I'm going to miss you."

His hands stilled against her then he squeezed her so tight she could barely draw breath. "I'll miss you, too."

Landon released her and walked away, taking long strides toward the house. Rascal darted across the front lawn and followed him.

Katie bit her lip, her heart breaking into a thousand pieces. For Landon. For the kids. For Jennifer and Frank. And for herself.

"Landon?"

He paused and glanced over his shoulder.

"Thank you for helping me," she said softly.

Landon smiled, but it was empty and sad. "Take care of them, Katie."

Chapter 11

Katie clicked a button on the remote in her hand, advancing the slideshow presentation to the last image, then faced the small group of men and women seated around the mahogany table in KC Marketing's Los Angeles boardroom.

"And this," she said, "is the packaging Sandra has chosen for the bath boutique products. As you can see, the frills on the wrapping are minimal and the most care and attention has gone into producing eye-catching yet elegant lettering. These boutique products are high quality and their performance speaks for itself, so Sandra and I agreed last week that fancy packaging wasn't necessary. Instead, the emphasis for the Sandra's Sexy Suds brand will be on the quality of the product rather than gimmicky sales tricks or the flash-in-the-pan promotions our competitors employ. We're seeking to build a loyal clientele."

Sandra, seated at the opposite end of the table, nodded. "I couldn't be more pleased with what Katie has done. And I truly believe her marketing approach will help consumers see how special our product is and keep them coming back for more."

"And you're confident that no improvements are needed to the formula prior to distribution?" Carla Lemming, Katie's boss and head of KC Marketing, rubbed her chin thoughtfully.

"Very confident." Katie spread her hands, trying her best not to glance at the window for the hundredth time. It was dark out and she'd already stayed two hours later than she'd anticipated. "I've tested every item myself."

Carla smiled. "Then I'd say this is a go. Nice job, Katie."

"Thank you." Katie turned off the projector and checked her watch. Her stomach dropped. It was already eight o'clock. "If there are no more questions, we're all done here."

And not a moment too soon. Katie had promised Matthew and Emma that she'd be home over two hours ago.

Everyone stood, expressed their approval then left the boardroom, smiling, shaking hands and chatting along the way. Except for Carla and Sandra. Both lingered in the boardroom, examining the products on the table and thanking Katie for her hard work.

"I'm so happy with your plans," Sandra said, admiring one of the boutique gift baskets Katie had put together.

"I was happy to help." Katie sneaked another glance at her watch.

"I'd like to meet with you in the morning, Katie." Carla picked up a bath bomb and rolled it around in her palm. "We just signed a new client and I think you'd be perfect for his project. Think you could come in an hour early tomorrow?"

Katie winced. "I'd love to, but I thought I'd take a break. Maybe put in for a few days off?"

"A break?" Carla made a face. "In all the years we've worked together, I don't recall you ever taking a break." Her face flushed. "Well, except for..."

Carla looked down, her voice trailing off, but there was no need for her to finish. *The funerals* were what she'd meant to say. The one time Katie had taken time off work had been two and a half weeks ago when she'd returned to Elk Valley for Jennifer's and Frank's funerals.

"I'm sorry," Carla said. "I didn't mean—"

Katie held up a hand. "No. It's okay. But I do have more obligations than I used to, and it would be a big help if I could take the time off."

Carla's smile returned. "Of course. Take a few days." She headed for the door then hesitated on the threshold. "But, Katie?"

"Yes?"

Carla's mouth twisted. "If you're still interested in the new executive position, I think I should let you know now that the demands of the job—time-wise—will be even greater."

Katie nodded slowly. "I understand."

After Carla left, Sandra whistled. "Wow. There is no mincing of words with her, is there?"

Katie shrugged. "She's straightforward. Always has been. I used to like that about her."

"And now?"

Katie toyed with three of the bath bombs in front of her, arranging them in a line, and avoided Sandra's eyes. "I don't know. I guess I'm just not as…enthusiastic about work as I used to be."

Sandra hesitated then asked, "Because of the kids?"

"Yeah." Katie looked at her watch again, her shoulders slumping. "It's only been a week and a half but I can already tell I can't keep the same hours I used to."

"You can't?" Sandra asked softly. "Or you don't want to?"

Katie stilled, her fingers resting on the pink bath bomb at the end of the row she'd formed. The last one she'd named using Landon's suggestion.

Be in Love.

"I don't know," Katie whispered. "I just know that by the time I make it home at night, the kids are either already in the bed or about to be." She forced a laugh. "If my mom hadn't flown in yesterday for the weekend and offered to babysit for free tonight, I would've paid babysitters more than I made this month, and other than taking Matthew and Emma to the beach their first day after moving here, I've broken every promise I've made to spend more time with them."

Sandra sighed. "I'm sorry, Katie."

"I knew things would change," Katie continued. "But I didn't know—" She lifted her arms, at a loss for words. "I guess, I didn't know that…"

"That *you* would change, too?"

Katie stared at Sandra. "Maybe." After a moment,

she opened her bag, swept the bath bombs in it then headed for the door. Katie hugged Sandra on her way out. "I've got to go. I'm already late."

She drove back to her apartment as quickly as she could while still making it there in one piece. The elevator was broken—again—so she took the stairs, jogging up them two at a time until she reached her floor. Outside the door, she paused to catch her breath, smooth her hair and pin a smile on her face.

Which was a sign in and of itself. Used to be, she'd looked forward to putting her feet up after a hard day's work, but now she felt guilty every time she walked in the door.

Taking a deep breath, Katie went in and smiled wide at her mother and the kids, who sat around the small kitchen table. "I'm home."

Katie cringed. The words had sounded as lackluster out loud as they had in her head.

Matthew and Emma looked up, both picking at a mostly uneaten plate of food, waved a hand in the air then stared back down at the table.

"We held dinner as long as we could for you." Patricia scooped the last bit of pureed peas from a jar and fed it to Sophia. "About a half hour ago, the kids became too hungry to wait any longer."

Katie walked into the kitchen, placed her purse on the table and sat beside Sophia. "I'm sorry. I really am. I tried my best to get out of there sooner."

Matthew put down his fork. "It's okay, Aunt Katie."

"No. It's not." Katie's throat tightened as she looked at Sophia, who smiled back at her from a high chair. "I promised you I'd be home earlier than this and I didn't follow through. *Again.*" Turning back to Matthew, she forced a smile. "How was school today?"

He looked away and picked at a loose thread on the tablecloth.

"Matthew?" Katie leaned closer and placed a hand on his shoulder. "I'd like to hear how your day w—"

"I don't know anybody, okay?" Chin trembling, he shook his head. "None of my friends are here and the classes are different."

"In what way? If you'd like me to, I could speak to your teachers."

"It won't help." Matthew frowned, his voice lowering to a whisper. "I like Elk Valley Elementary better. And I miss my video games. I forgot and left them behind."

"Well, we can get you new video games." Katie bit her lip. "Emma? What about you? How was your day?"

Emma continued staring at the table.

"Emma?"

"I miss Uncle Landon."

Emma's words were so soft, Katie barely caught them. But she did, and before she realized it, Katie whispered back, "I miss him, too."

Matthew and Emma looked up at her, a hopeful look on their faces.

Katie's eyes burned. She rubbed her forehead then held out her arms. "It's getting late. How 'bout a quick hug before you take your baths? I even brought some bath bubbles back for you."

They both stood and hugged her then went to their rooms, the same crestfallen looks on their faces that they'd sported the majority of the past week, leaving Katie to feel guiltier than ever.

"What's wrong with me, Mom?" Katie slumped back in her chair and bit back a sob. "Why can't I get this right?"

Patricia began stacking the dirty dishes. "It's early yet. The kids have only been here a little over a week, and you're doing your best."

"But my best isn't good enough." Katie shook her head. "I promised them so much and I haven't delivered any of it. And why are you defending me?" She managed a smile despite her low spirits. "It's kind of creeping me out. I'm used to you critiquing me, not cutting me slack."

Patricia laughed then put down the dishes and sat beside her. "That last part is absolutely true. I have been too hard on you and it's something I'm trying to rectify now." She squeezed Katie's shoulder. "Believe me when I say no one is perfect, Katie. If you need an example, look at us. All of those years I could've built a close relationship with you and instead, I let my resentment get in the way."

Katie stilled. "Resentment?"

"Yes." Patricia sighed. "Please don't misunderstand me—I didn't blame you for wanting to branch out and leave Elk Valley—but I was hurt by how quickly you left. It felt as though you couldn't wait to get away from all of us. What hurt even more was that you rarely ever came home. It was like you'd forgotten us."

"That wasn't it." Katie twisted her hands in her lap. "I just didn't feel like I fit in Elk Valley. When I came here, I found a successful job, made new friends and this place felt like home." She glanced around at her apartment, realizing how much she missed her small mountain hometown, the ranch and…Landon. "I've been chasing so many things over the years, I don't think I've ever stopped to think about what I really wanted out of life, and what I have here doesn't feel like home anymore."

"What does feel like home?" Patricia asked, a note of hope in her voice.

Katie smiled. "Elk Valley. I miss you and Dad." *And Landon.* "I miss leading chorus practice at the elementary school and being called Ms. Richards. I even miss mucking the stalls in Landon's stable." She curled her hands around her purse, feeling the bath bombs she'd tossed in there beneath her fingertips. Her smile grew. "I don't want a promotion here in California. I want to find a job closer to Elk Valley where I can be at home more. I want to spend more time with Matthew, Emma and Sophia. I want to take them camping and sing with them at festivals, laugh more often and play like a kid myself once in a while on the weekends. And I want to—" Her voice broke and she swallowed hard. "I want to be in love. Every day."

Patricia squeezed her shoulder tighter. "With Landon?"

Katie met her eyes. "Yes."

"Well, now that you know what you want," Patricia said, grinning, "what are you waiting for?"

Landon pushed off the porch rail with his foot, rocked back in his rocking chair and stifled a frustrated sigh for what felt like the millionth time.

He glanced around his familiar surroundings and breathed in the warm spring air. The stars were out and the moon, though not full, shone almost as bright. That same ol' barred owl hooted among the rustles of the trees. And the towering range of mountains impressed themselves upon the valley as usual.

But something had changed. Something was off.

Landon glanced at Rascal, who sprawled on the porch floor by his side, blinking up at him silently. Then he stared at the smooth, empty driveway. One without a rut in sight.

Groaning, he shoved the rocking chair back and stood, glancing over his shoulder as the headrest thumped against the side of the house.

That's what was missing. It was too quiet. Too still.

He left the porch and went inside. Walked to the kitchen, grabbed a beer from the fridge, cracked the top off then upended it. He leaned against the sink, took a few swallows and looked around the room, but his house remained just as quiet, just as still and just as empty.

Rascal scampered into the kitchen, sniffed around then lay down and lowered his head onto his paws.

"I know," Landon whispered. "I miss them, too."

He had every day for over a week now and would probably miss them every day for the foreseeable future.

A smile pulled at his mouth as he stared at the high chair across the room. He wondered what sweet Sophia was doing now. He glanced at the clock on the wall. Katie had probably given her a bath, rocked her to sleep and settled her in her crib.

And Emma? She'd be brushing her teeth right about now, piling up in the bed and waiting for a bedtime story. Matthew wouldn't be too far behind, either. If he had his video games, he'd more than likely be try-ing to sneak in a few extra minutes, but as he'd left his console behind on the entertainment stand, there was little chance of that. And with the kids settled in bed for the night, Katie would probably be headed for her tub and a long soak in a bubble bath.

Landon set his beer bottle on the table and dragged a hand over his face. No more alcohol tonight. It was making him maudlin.

He left the kitchen and trudged through the living room, stumbling to a halt in front of the TV. Speaking of video games, there it was. That damned aggravating contraption Matthew had left behind. Though, Landon had to admit, the idea of a noisy distraction filling the house was too good to pass up.

Landon turned on the TV and the game console, grabbed a controller then sat on the floor. Colorful images flickered across the screen and the familiar loud pings of the game clamored through the air. He flicked the joystick with his thumb and had no clue what he was doing, but the sights and sounds alone were enough to ease the throbbing pain inside him.

God, he missed the kids. And Katie. He missed Katie so damned much.

The floorboards behind him creaked. "Landon?"

Heart stalling, he paused the game and jumped to his feet.

Amber stood just inside the doorway, eyeing him with concern. "I knocked but I guess you didn't hear me."

His shoulders sagged but he straightened and tried to hide his disappointment. "Sorry." He was happy to see his sister—he really was. At the moment, he just wished she was someone else. "I was, uh—" he motioned over his shoulder "—just playing a game."

A small smile flickered across Amber's mouth. "I see that."

"Is everything okay? The triplets all right?"

"Oh, yeah." Amber waved away his concern. "Nate's with them. I just gave a friend a ride and your place happened to be on the way, so I thought I'd stop by and check on you. See if you needed anything?"

Landon managed a smile. "That's supposed to be my line, isn't it?"

"Maybe." Amber shrugged. "But I can be concerned about my big brother once in a while, right?"

He nodded. "I'm fine."

She gestured toward the TV. "But lonely, huh?"

"Yeah." He rubbed the back of his neck. "I miss them."

"I have a feeling that'll get better soon." Before he could respond, Amber walked over, kissed his cheek then headed for the door. "Nate's been alone with the kids for an hour now, so he's probably desperate for me to show back up. Call me if you need anything."

He made to answer but she had already left, her light footsteps fading down the front steps. A door slammed, and an engine cranked then the sound of a car receded into the distance, leaving the ranch quiet again.

Landon frowned—the house felt emptier than ever—and was just turning back to the game when a knock sounded on the front door.

"You forget something?" He strode across the living room and opened the screen door, but instead of his blonde, five-and-a-half-foot sister, he found a stroller with a twenty-five-inch-tall baby with brown curls and the damned cutest grin he'd ever seen.

"Sophia?"

Her eyes widened at the sight of him and she chortled, her chubby arms reaching for him.

Landon picked her up, lifting her against his chest just as Rascal scampered out and barked with excitement.

"Uncle Landon!" Footsteps pounded up the front steps then Matthew and Emma ran onto the porch, hurled themselves against him and wrapped their arms around his thighs.

"What in the world?" Landon stumbled back, grinning like a loon and hugging them tight with his free arm.

Both his arms and his heart were full to overflowing, but then he noticed someone else standing at the foot of the steps, smiling up at him and making every nerve ending in his body shoot to attention.

"Katie," he said, voice husky.

"Good." She smiled. "I was hoping you'd be home." Her voice sounded sweeter than he remembered.

Katie waved a thin stack of papers in the air. "There's something I want to talk to you about."

Landon shook his head. "What's that?"

"Loose ends." She climbed the steps, her long brown hair swinging over her shoulders, and her dark eyes warmed as they focused on his face. "Matthew, will you please take your sisters inside so I can talk to Landon for a minute?"

"Yes, ma'am." Matthew helped Landon settle Sophia back in the stroller then Matthew and Emma wheeled it inside the house and shut the door.

Landon watched Katie closely, tamping down the

eager hope rising within him. "What loose ends are you talking about?"

"The ones concerning us." Katie stopped in front of him, her gaze roving over his frame eagerly as she leaned in slightly. As though she may have missed him as much as he'd missed her.

He held his breath. "Why aren't you in California?"

"Because you're not there."

He smiled, his whole body warming.

"You see…" Katie held up the papers. "I got to reading this custody arrangement and I studied all the fine print concerning primary and secondary guardianship and noticed that there was one variable Jennifer and Frank didn't actually spell out in the will or in Jennifer's letter."

His smile faded. "What variable?"

"The one where I fell in love with you." She stepped closer, the shy look in her eyes giving her a vulnerable air. "The one where I missed you and couldn't stand being apart from you. The one where I only felt at home when I was with you on this ranch. And I started thinking that if I were to ask you to marry me and you said yes, then we would be equal guardians. Equal partners, that is. But—" Her voice faltered and her chest lifted on a deep breath. "But there's one condition. The only way this new kind of partnership will work is if you're in love with me, too."

He studied her face. Noticed the slight shaking in her hands. "So if I'm not in love with you, I can't accept your proposal?"

"That's the condition. This can only be about love, not logic or convenience."

He frowned. "You've been talking to my sister about me, haven't you?"

Her cheeks flushed. "Maybe. So...do you love me?"

Landon narrowed his eyes. "I have one question."

Her bottom lip trembled. "What's that?"

"We split my bathroom—including the tub—fifty-fifty?"

She nodded.

Landon grinned. "I love you, Katie. Always will."

Excitement and happiness lit up her expression and her attention drifted toward his smile. "So that's a yes?"

Landon reached out and tugged her close, whispering just before he kissed her, "That's a hell yes."

Katie smiled against his lips then kissed him back. Her soft sigh of pleasure and the children's laughter from inside their home were the sweetest sounds Landon had ever heard.

* * * * *

*Alyssa Santangelo has no memory of the
past seven years—including her divorce—but she
remembers her love for Connor Bravo. One way
or another, she's going to get her husband back.*

*Read on for a sneak preview of
A Husband She Couldn't Forget,
the next book in Christine Rimmer's
The Bravos of Valentine Bay miniseries.*

An accident. I've been in an accident. The stitches they'd
put in her knee throbbed dully, her cheeks and forehead
burned and she had a mild headache. Every time she took
a breath, she remembered that the seat belt had not been
very nice to her.

She must have made a noise, because as she sagged
back to the pillow again, Dante flinched and opened
his eyes. "Hey, little sis." He'd always called her that,
even though she was second eldest, after him. "How you
feelin'?"

"Everything aches," she grumbled. "But I'll live."
Longing flooded her for the comfort of her husband's
strong arms. She needed him near. He would soothe all
her pains and ease her weird, formless fears. "Where's
Connor gotten off to?"

Dante's mouth fell half-open, as though in bafflement at her question. "Connor?"

He looked so befuddled, she couldn't help chuckling a little, even though laughing made her chest and ribs hurt. "Yeah. Connor. You know, that guy I married nine years ago—my husband, your brother-in-law?"

Dante sat up. He also continued to gape at her like she was a few screwdrivers short of a full tool kit. "Uh, what's going on? You think you're funny?"

"Funny? Because I want my husband?" She bounced back up to a sitting position. "What exactly is happening here? I mean it, Dante. Be straight with me. Where's Connor?"

Don't miss
A Husband She Couldn't Forget
by Christine Rimmer,
available October 2019 wherever
Harlequin® Special Edition books and ebooks are sold.

www.Harlequin.com

Looking for more satisfying love stories
with community and family at their core?

Check out **Harlequin® Special Edition**
and **Love Inspired®** books!

New books available every month!

Looking for inspiration in tales
of hope, faith and heartfelt romance?

Check out **Love Inspired**® and
Love Inspired® **Suspense** books!

New books available every month!

CONNECT WITH US AT:

Facebook.com/groups/HarlequinConnection

Facebook.com/HarlequinBooks

Twitter.com/HarlequinBooks

Instagram.com/HarlequinBooks

Pinterest.com/HarlequinBooks

ReaderService.com

LIGENRE2018R2

SPECIAL EXCERPT FROM

Love Inspired®

*Could a pretend Christmastime courtship
lead to a forever match?*

Read on for a sneak preview of
Her Amish Holiday Suitor, *part of Carrie Lighte's
Amish Country Courtships miniseries.*

Nick took his seat next to her and picked up the reins, but before moving onward, he said, "I don't understand it, Lucy. Why is my caring about you such an awful thing?" His voice was quivering and Lucy felt a pang of guilt. She knew she was overreacting. Rather, she was reacting to a heartache that had plagued her for years, not one Nick had caused that evening.

"I don't expect you to understand," she said, wiping her rough woolen mitten across her cheeks.

"But I want to. Can't you explain it to me?"

Nick's voice was so forlorn Lucy let her defenses drop. "I've always been treated like this, my entire life. *Lucy's too weak, too fragile, too small, she can't go outside or run around or have any fun because she'll get sick. She'll stop breathing. She'll wind up in the hospital.* My whole life, Nick. And then the one little taste of utter abandon I ever experienced—charging through the dark with a frosty wind whisking against my face, feeling totally invigorated and alive… You want to take that away from me, too."

She was crying so hard her words were barely intelligible, but Nick didn't interrupt or attempt to quiet her. When she finally settled down and could speak normally again, she sniffed and asked, "May I use your handkerchief, please?"

"Sorry, I don't have one," Nick said. "But here, you can use my scarf. I don't mind."

The offer to use Nick's scarf to dry her eyes and blow her nose was so ridiculous and sweet all at once it caused Lucy to chuckle. "*Neh*, that's okay," she said, removing her mittens to dab her eyes with her bare fingers.

"I really am sorry," he repeated.

Lucy was embarrassed. "That's all right. I've stopped blubbering. I don't need a handkerchief after all."

"*Neh*, I mean I'm sorry I treated you in a way that made you feel…the way you feel. I didn't mean to. I was concerned. I care about you and I wouldn't want anything to happen to you. I especially wouldn't want to play a role in hurting you."

Lucy was overwhelmed by his words. No man had ever said anything like that to her before, even in friendship. "It's not your fault," she said. "And I do appreciate that you care. But I'm not as fragile as you think I am."

"Fragile? You? I don't think you're fragile at all, even if you are prone to pneumonia." Nick scoffed. "I think you're one of the most resilient women I've ever known."

Lucy was overwhelmed again. If this kept up, she was going to fall hard for Nick Burkholder. Maybe she already had.

Don't miss
Her Amish Holiday Suitor *by Carrie Lighte,*
available October 2019 wherever
Love Inspired® books and ebooks are sold.

www.LoveInspired.com

Love Harlequin romance?

DISCOVER.

Be the first to find out about promotions, news and exclusive content!

f Facebook.com/HarlequinBooks

𝕏 Twitter.com/HarlequinBooks

◉ Instagram.com/HarlequinBooks

𝐏 Pinterest.com/HarlequinBooks

ReaderService.com

EXPLORE.

Sign up for the Harlequin e-newsletter and download a free book from any series at **TryHarlequin.com**.

CONNECT.

Join our Harlequin community to share your thoughts and connect with other romance readers!
Facebook.com/groups/HarlequinConnection

Reward the book lover in you!

Earn points on your purchase of new Harlequin books from participating retailers.

Turn your points into **FREE BOOKS** of your choice!

Join for FREE today at
www.HarlequinMyRewards.com.

Harlequin My Rewards is a free program (no fees) without any commitments or obligations.

MYR18